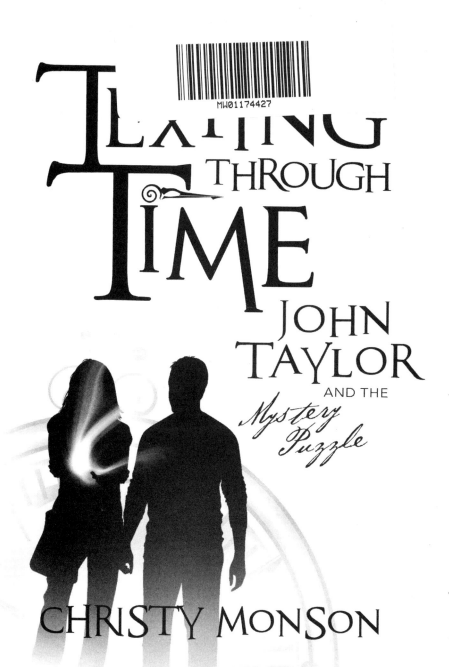

Playing THROUGH Time

JOHN TAYLOR

AND THE

Mystery Puzzle

CHRISTY MONSON

Bonneville Books
An Imprint of Cedar Fort, Inc.
Springville, Utah

TO CHILDREN OF GOD
EVERYWHERE

© 2012 Christy Monson

The views expressed within this work are the sole responsibility of the author and do not necessarily reflect the position of Cedar Fort, Inc., or any other entity.

This is a work of fiction. The characters, names, incidents, places, and dialogue are products of the author's imagination, and are not to be construed as real.

ISBN 13: 978-1-4621-1084-1

Published by Bonneville Books, an imprint of Cedar Fort, Inc.
2373 W. 700 S., Springville, UT 84663
Distributed by Cedar Fort, Inc. www.cedarfort.com

LIBRARY OF CONGRESS CATALOGING-IN-PUBLICATION DATA

Monson, Christy, 1942-
  John Taylor and the mystery puzzle / Christy Monson.
    p. cm.
  Includes bibliographical references and index.
  ISBN 978-1-4621-1084-1 (alk. paper)
  1. Brothers and sisters--Fiction. 2. Taylor, John, 1808-1887--Fiction. 3. Time travel--Fiction. 4. Cell phones--Fiction. I. Title.
  PS3613.O5383J64 2012
  813'.6--dc23
                                        2012032979

Cover design by Erica Dixon
Cover design © 2012 by Lyle Mortimer
Illustrations by Rose Ledezma
Edited and typeset by Whitney A. Lindsley

Printed in the United States of America

10 9 8 7 6 5 4 3 2 1

FOREWORD

THE life of John Taylor, the third president of The Church of Jesus Christ of Latter-day Saints, has long been in need of reflection and attention by LDS authors. Faith, strength, and an example worth emulating can be gleaned from such a study. In *Texting Through Time: John Taylor and the Mystery Puzzle*, Christy Monson has brought to the middle-grade reader a wonderful view of this prophet. Creating a word-journey through time, she has introduced a new generation to this prophet of God.

Thoroughly researching the life of John Taylor, Monson has based her story on historical evidence, representing the best in juvenile historical fiction. Through captivating conversations, she captures for her readers the essence of President Taylor's life and personality. Using modern technology as a backdrop, Monson introduces her relatable characters to text-savvy viewers. She includes magical interludes to keep a young audience's attention, while skillfully interlacing scriptures throughout the story line. Descriptive language guides readers through England, Canada, Nauvoo, Winter Quarters, Salt Lake City, and France; but, more important it takes readers through various incidents involved in the making of a prophet of God.

Beginning the book with an event where John Taylor and his older brother battle imaginary Scots, a young reader is immediately enthralled. A Latter-day Saint youth reading this book is shown the great courage of John Taylor, who would later hide in a granary to uphold the laws of God. Monson captures John Taylor's personality and habits, even hinting at his fastidious dress, which was manifest in the mannerly culture in which he was raised. Of particular interest is the handling of Joseph Smith's martyrdom as she reveals that John Taylor was one who would lay his life down for a friend.

This novelette covers all aspects of John Taylor's life including his professions, faith, and family experiences. Monson shows Taylor as being a strict parent, including into the plot an incident where John Taylor made his sons pay fourfold for errant chickens a neighbor had given them. At the same time, she shows him as a tender parent, who forbids his son to read Jules Verne's *Twenty-Thousand Leagues Under the Sea* and then stayed up all night reading it himself. President Taylor then admits he has made a mistake, and allows his son to read Verne's novel. Revealing President Taylor's sense of humor, she includes an episode where one of his sons skipped church and was told by a friend that an "Old Wind Bag" had spoken at the meeting. Hearing of the report, President Taylor laughed and told his son that he indeed was the "Old Wind Bag"

With these examples and many more, any modern LDS youth reading this volume will not only learn of John Taylor, but may also strive to emulate that personality and example into their own lives.

MARY JANE WOODGER

JUST FOR FUN

MICAH slumped against the big rock in front of his house while his sister Alicia lounged on the grass nearby. He rubbed his left ankle, which he had twisted in the touch football game last night. A trickle of sweat slipped down into his ear. "Why does it have to be so hot?"

"I don't know," said Alicia. "I wish we lived someplace cool."

"Remember in Primary Sister Wilson told us how green and beautiful England is?" The drop of sweat tickled, so he wiped it out.

"Wasn't that the lesson about John Taylor?" asked Alicia. "That's where he grew up."

"Right," said Micah, smiling. "Wanna go there?"

"No way," said Alicia.

"Come on," said Micah. "I have an idea."

"Oh, no," said Alicia. "I don't like it when you get that look in your eyes. The last time that happened we ended up trapped in the past."

"We weren't trapped," said Micah. "We just didn't know how to work the phone."

"I did love being with Brigham Young, though," said Alicia.

"Let's do it again." Micah shifted himself to a more comfortable position against the rock. A pinecone from the tree above plopped onto his head.

Alicia giggled. "It's a sign you're gonna get us into trouble again."

Micah rubbed his head. "Owww." It didn't really hurt, but he had to make it look like it did. "Let's go ask Dad if we can take the phone again."

"He's never going to let us do that," said Alicia, twisting her necklace around her finger.

"Doesn't hurt to ask. Besides, I'm thirteen now. He'll trust me." Micah jumped up and headed for the house.

Alicia raced beside him. "He'll tell you it's not safe."

"No, he won't," said Micah.

"Yes, he will," said Alicia.

Micah burst in the back door and hurried to the den. "Dad, can we use the phone to go to England?"

"What?" asked Dad, shuffling some papers on his desk. "England? Why on earth would you want to go to England?"

"It's where John Taylor was born," said Micah.

"The phone's not safe," said Dad. "Surely you remember that."

Micah glanced at Alicia, who smirked. He hated it when she was right.

Dad leaned forward in his desk chair and picked up the phone. "I put a new back on it so it'll stay closed, and I've started reprogramming it with some new upgrades, so it'll work a little differently. But I really need to study the log files to make sure there are no more problems."

"There aren't any problems with the phone," said Micah. "It works just fine. The only glitch was me not knowing to press the PRESENT button to get back home, and I can do that now."

"The phone still needs a thorough going-over before we know it's really safe." Dad swiped his thumb over the keypad. "To start with, why don't you check the battery?" He handed Micah the phone. "The charger's at the office. I'll take it in when I go on Monday." Dad turned back to his papers on the desk.

Micah switched the phone on. "It's low, two out of five bars, but that's okay. We just want to see the place John Taylor grew up, and then we'll come right back home. It'll be a really good experience for me. I'm sure he had to work hard, and I'll learn more about helping and putting in extra effort."

Dad straightened the papers on his desk again. "I don't know."

Alicia crossed her eyes, jabbed her finger toward her throat and pretended to gag. "You're sure full of yourself," she whispered to Micah.

Micah smiled and stuck his tongue out at her. He knew Alicia could see right through him. Sometimes she was too sassy for her own good.

"Just one scene, pleeease," said Micah.

Alicia raised her eyebrows.

"Not safe until I check it out thoroughly," said Dad.

Micah hung his head and clenched his fists. Why wouldn't Dad listen?

Dad put his hand on Micah's shoulder. "I'm sorry, son."

"I have an idea," said Alicia. "How about you come with us, Dad?"

Micah's face lit up. "Great! That way you can fix the phone if there's a problem."

"Well," said Dad, rubbing his hand over his chin. "It sounds like you had a really good time visiting Brigham Young, and I might like a trip back to 1800 England myself."

"Let's go," said Micah, pulling up the PAST, PRESENT, and FUTURE screen.

"Wait," said Dad. "Right this minute?"

"Sure," said Micah.

"I should at least tell your mother where we're going." Dad hurried from the room.

Micah smiled to himself, breathing a sigh of relief. *This will be a stress-free trip*, he thought. *I won't have to worry about any problems with the phone.*

"Wow," said Alicia. "It'll be cool to have Dad with us."

Dad returned. "This will be great. I'm ready."

Micah hit the PAST button. BIOGRAPHY lit up below it. Micah typed JOHN TAYLOR, THIRD PROPHET OF THE CHURCH OF JESUS CHRIST OF LATTER-DAY SAINTS, and then selected BOYHOOD.

A black breeze swirled around them into the grayness of time. Micah floated, weightless, tumbling over and over. He grabbed Alicia's hand, and she held on. "You with us, Dad?"

"Noooooooo," came Dad's voice, fading into the distance.

"Uh-oh," said Micah. He couldn't see anything in the darkness. The fog blew away, and the tumbling changed to flying. He looked around, but Dad wasn't there. The ocean rolled below him. Salty air stung his eyes and nose. "We've lost Dad, and I don't know how to go back to get him."

"Can't you turn us around?" asked Alicia above the sound of the wind.

Micah tried to turn back, but he couldn't. He was moving forward too fast. What had happened? The phone always kept him and Alicia together. Why didn't it keep Dad with them? Now what would they do?

"There's an island down there," said Alicia. "I guess that's England."

Micah sighed. "England, here we come—without Dad."

They drifted toward the ground as if they wore parachutes and toppled onto the grass.

CUMBRIA (WESTMORELAND), ENGLAND, AUGUST 1820 appeared on the phone's screen.

"Try asking the phone about Dad," said Alicia.

Micah typed, WHAT HAPPENED TO DAD?

The phone lit up: MICAH AND ALICIA, RECOGNIZED USERS

"Does that mean it won't take anyone but us?" asked Alicia.

"I guess," said Micah, "but Dad is the one who created the program."

"Let me see the phone," said Alicia. TAKE US HOME TO GET DAD, she typed.

MICAH AND ALICIA, RECOGNIZED USERS remained on the screen, followed by JOURNEY ACTIVATED. BEGIN.

5

"Maybe Dad isn't a recognized user," said Alicia.

"I don't understand," said Micah, "but I guess we have no choice."

"Things aren't going well so far, and it doesn't look like we can go back," Alicia said, pointing to the message on the screen.

"I suppose we just go on like we did with Brigham," said Micah, a sinking feeling filling his stomach. "Let's make the best of it." He stood up and brushed off his pants. At least he had shoes and socks on. That was better than Brigham Young's time. Looking down at his shirt, he shuddered in disbelief. "I have a lace collar and . . ."

"Blousy sleeves," giggled Alicia, touching his arm. "I would much sooner have a shirt like yours than this plain long dress. I wish I had my shorts on. Ugh! And my CTR ring is gone."

"I'd rather have your short sleeves than this girl's blouse," said Micah. *Oh well*, he thought. *I guess this is what they wore.*

"Your shirt is untucked," said Alicia.

"I don't care." Micah looked at the green rolling hills around him. Stone fences and hedges separated the fields. Sheep grazed on the lush green grass. "Only farmers live here anyway, and I'm sure they don't tuck their shirts in."

"Look," said Alicia, pointing, "there's a crumbling castle at the top of that hill. I want to go up there."

Suddenly three boys charged past them, running the other way. "To the pele tower,"[1] one of them shouted. They had on the same kind of clothes Micah wore.

"The Scots are coming," another yelled.

"Slay them with your swords," the last boy shouted. "Call in King Arthur and the Knights of the Round Table. Charge . . ."

War, thought Micah. *I love to play War.* "They're headed to that tower over there. Let's follow them."

"But I want to go to the castle," said Alicia.

"We'll go there next, promise," said Micah. "First, to the tower."

Alicia and Micah ran after the boys. Ahead stood a tall, square rock tower with no windows surrounded by battlements at the top.

"Why does the wall around the roof have cutouts in it? Didn't they have enough rocks to finish it?" asked Alicia.

Micah rolled his eyes. Girls didn't understand anything about war. "Those are not cutouts. The taller sections are battlements to protect soldiers during the battle. They shoot their arrows through the cutouts."

The boys scrambled into a partially crumbling tower. Micah peeked into the doorway. "Wow, the walls are thicker than we are tall."

Alicia shoved past him into the room. "Ewww, are those the bones of a dead soldier in the corner?"

Micah followed. "It looks like an animal's leg bone to me." He kicked it out of the way. A staircase led up to the next floor. Micah scrambled up the stone steps with Alicia right behind him. A tin cup and spoon lay in the rubble near the outside wall.

"I'll bet this was the kitchen," said Alicia.

"Who cares where the kitchen was," said Micah. "To the battle!" He headed up the stairs to the next floor.

"More piles of rocks," said Alicia. "Is this the

bedroom? Do you think this is where they slept?"

Girls, thought Micah. *What does it matter where the bedroom was?* He raced up the stairs to the roof, and Alicia followed.

"The army is coming!" shouted one of the boys. "To the battlements! Prepare your bows and arrows!"

"Uh, hi," said Micah.

The boys turned around. "Hello," said a boy with brown hair. "Do you want to play?"

"Sure," said Micah.

"I'm John Taylor," said the boy. He pointed to the two other boys. "This is my older brother, Edward, and our friend William Smith."

"I'm Micah, and this is my sister Alicia."

"Micah's a biblical name from the Old Testament," said John. "Is your family religious?"

"Yes," said Micah, worrying about more questions from John. He didn't want to tell them they were from the future.

"Are you from around here?"

"No, we're just here for the day."

"Visiting?" asked John.

"Yes," said Micah. *Whew, that was easy*, he thought.

Edward turned to William. "Tuck your shirt in. Father says we should always look presentable."

William tucked his shirt in.

Micah looked down at his shirt and frowned. He shoved it into his pants.

William patted John's arm and whispered loud enough for Micah to hear. "No girls allowed."

"But she's with me," said Micah. He hoped she'd stay for the battle. He really wanted to play.

John glanced at William. "She can play if she wants. But there are juicy ripe blackberries over by the castle wall." John pointed.

"Thanks, I'll go to the castle," said Alicia.

John smiled at Alicia. "Mother made us a scrumptious lunch." He patted his backpack. "We'll come eat in the castle with you in a little while, as soon as the battle's over."

Alicia turned and ran down the stairs.

"I'll come in a few minutes," Micah called after her, but she was gone. A guilty lump settled itself into his stomach. *John is more considerate of Alicia than I am,* thought Micah, and *Alicia is* my *sister. I should be more caring.*

"Defend the town!" shouted John.

Micah took his place at the battle station.

Alicia lifted her long skirt so she wouldn't trip and jumped down the stairs of the pele tower two at a time. Out the door and up the hill toward the crumbled castle ruins she raced. "I'm glad I didn't have to stay and play War," she said to the little blackbird on the hedge. "Shooting pretend arrows through little cutouts isn't my idea of fun."

Jagged stone walls decayed in peaks at the top of the hill. Alicia reached the ruins and climbed over the rocks blocking the doorway. She scrambled up on top of a collapsing wall to look over the entire valley of rolling hills and grazing sheep. Across the castle courtyard stood a rock outline of several rooms, but the walls were gone.

Alicia jumped down off the mound and ran to the largest area. She pictured a ballroom with fancy decorations and a large chandelier lit with candles. In her imagination, she could see elegant ladies, wearing fancy dresses and lots of jewelry, talking to each other. They began to dance, moving about the room to the music of an orchestra seated at one end. She bowed to the dancers and picked up the edge of her skirt and twirled around and around. One of the noble women draped a diamond necklace over her head, and she swirled between the dancers, noticing their earrings, tiaras, and rings. One of the fanciest ladies had on a glittery golden chain with a diamond flower in the center. Another wore a long string of pearls.

Just outside the tumble of rocks, Alicia noticed the blackberry bushes John had told her about. She left the music and dancing and climbed over the rubble to the berries. Big, ripe fruit hung from the thorny branches. Alicia reached in carefully, plucked one, and popped it in her mouth. As she bit down, sweet juice exploded on her tongue. What a treat!

She picked a handful of berries and climbed to the top of the wall. She pretended that a servant girl brought her a chair. "I'll have tea on the veranda with blackberry tarts," she told the girl.

"Yes, my lady." The girl curtseyed.

"Where are you?" came a voice from the hill below.

Alicia jumped. It was Micah.

"I'm up here!" she called. "Having tea on the veranda."

"Wow! This is fun," said Micah, scrambling up the rocks toward her. He should apologize to her because he didn't listen when she wanted to come here in the first place, but not with everyone around. He'd tell her later.

John, Edward, and William followed.

"Want to hear an echo?" asked William.

"Sure," said Alicia.

"Follow us," said William. He leaped from the wall and scurried through a crumbling doorway leading to stairs down into the ground.

The others followed into a narrow room with no windows. Alicia could see there used to be steps leading farther into the ground, probably to the cellar, but they had collapsed.

"Oooohhhh!" yelled Edward.

Sound bounced off the walls in every direction. Alicia covered her ears.

"Stop!" said William. "I'm showing them. It was my idea." He looked at Alicia. "We love the echo."

"Fine," said Edward. He was quiet.

Now William yelled, "Oooohhhh!" The sound echoed off the walls again.

"Too loud for me!" Alicia headed up the stairs and out the door. How could boys stand such shrill noises?

John followed her. "We'll share our lunch with you while you tell us where you came from. You have a funny accent." John pulled some blackberry-jam sandwiches out of his pack.

They looked good. Alicia took one. "Want to tell them where we came from?" she asked Micah as he poked his head out of the basement door.

"Sure," said Micah. "We have this magic tablet."

"We came from the future," interrupted Alicia.

"The future?" asked Edward. "How did you do that?"

"Magic belongs to the fairies and sprites and nymphs," said John. "I love reading about them, but they aren't real."

"Legends are just for kids," said Edward. "I want to know how magic helped you travel from the future."

"I believe in fairies," said William. "But I'm only eight. John is twelve, and Edward is fourteen. They're too old to believe."

John frowned at William. "I like magic and legends, but God is the one who gives us blessings."

"Let me see the magic tablet," said William. "Did you get it from the fairies?"

"No, we didn't get it from the fairies," said Micah.

This conversation is all mixed up, thought Alicia. *It's worse than the one with Brigham Young.* "It isn't really magic, like fairy-magic. There have been a lot of new inventions since your time, and we call it magic because we don't know how it works exactly." Alicia breathed out a frustrated sigh. There was no good way to explain about the phone.

"Can we see it?" asked John.

"Sure," said Micah.

The boys crowded around.

Micah pulled the phone out and turned it on. PAST, PRESENT, and FUTURE appeared on the screen.

"It doesn't look like it belongs to fairies," said William. "I want to try it." He poked the FUTURE button before Micah could stop him.

The phone crackled. UNRECOGNIZED USER PRINT flashed on the screen.

"Oh, no," said Micah, quickly pushing the PRESENT button.

A jagged slash cut the writing in half. The phone lit up with another message: USER PRINT RECOGNIZED.

The phone went blank, and blackness swirled around Micah and Alicia.

"We're going, even before our picnic," said Alicia, "and those sandwiches looked really good."

Micah and Alicia faded into grayness and were gone.

ANGELIC MUSIC

ALICIA and Micah landed near the shore of a beautiful lake next to a weeping willow tree with branches draping almost to the ground. *Where are we?* wondered Micah.

The sun shone and the water gently lapped at the shore.

"This is probably still England," said Alicia. "It's sure pretty."

The phone lit up: USER PRINT RECOGNIZED appeared again.

"Whew!" said Micah, feeling relieved. "At least the phone knows it's me."

"It's a very smart phone," said Alicia.

"It must have an automatic recognition system in it," said Micah.

"Well, what do we do now?" asked Alicia.

"Push PRESENT again," said Micah.

PAST, PRESENT, and FUTURE lit up across the screen. Micah pushed PRESENT.

TEXT YOUR JOURNALS HOME, the phone requested.

"No," said Micah, feeling irritated. He held the

phone in front of his face. "You're supposed to *take* us home. Dad is waiting for us, wondering where we are." He pushed PRESENT again.

TEXT YOUR JOURNALS HOME, the phone said.

"Oh, all right," grumbled Micah. "I didn't think we needed to do that. We were only going to see John's boyhood." But he smiled to himself. It was too beautiful a day to feel cross.

"The phone is in charge," said Alicia, "not us." She began pulling her shoes and stockings off. "I'm going to wade into the water. Look, it glistens like a bracelet with a thousand diamonds.

Micah smiled. *Alicia and her jewelry.*

He typed:

JOHN MUST BE FROM A RICH FAMILY. HE HAS SHIRTS WITH LACE COLLARS AND PUFFY SLEEVES. I HAD TO TUCK MY SHIRT IN. PLAYED WAR AGAINST THE SCOTS. FUN, FUN, FUN.

He hit SEND. "Look, we don't have to use the shortened texting words like we did with Brigham Young."

Alicia pulled her other sock off. Then she took the phone from Micah and typed:

JOHN IS KIND. HE TOLD ME TO PICK BLACKBERRIES. AND HE WANTED TO SHARE HIS LUNCH WITH ME. I LOVED THE CASTLE RUINS, ATE BERRIES, DREAMED OF BEAUTIFUL JEWEL NECKLACES. CASTLE ECHOES ARE TOO LOUD FOR ME. MISSED THE PICNIC AND JAM SANDWICHES.

She sent the message.

Micah took the phone back. Alicia wiggled her toes in the water.

The screen flashed. JUNE 1824, PENRITH, LAKES DISTRICT, CUMBRIA, ENGLAND.

Micah held the phone out in front of him again. "No, take us home. I pushed PRESENT."

JUNE 1824, PENRITH, LAKES DISTRICT, CUMBRIA, ENGLAND remained on the screen.

"Dad is waiting for us," said Micah, but the phone remained unchanged. What would they do now? Dread clutched at him. They couldn't get home. Were they trapped again?

"Well, Mr. Full-of-Yourself," said Alicia. "What do we do now?"

Micah's stomach felt like it dropped to his knees. "I don't know." The phone had a way of making him feel very humble. "I guess we find John and see what he's doing today."

Micah stood up and stretched his arms. He still had on the blousy shirt, and he made sure it was tucked in. The edges of Alicia's long skirt dipped into the water as she waded in the lake.

Micah looked around and noticed a path circling the hill above the lake. "Come on. Let's walk along that trail," said Micah.

"I'd rather explore those stone ruins over there," said Alicia.

"Where?" asked Micah.

"The ones covered with moss and green bushes," said Alicia, pointing.

"We'll do that later. I think we'd better find John and then try to get back home." He wasn't listening to Alicia again, but the pressure was on. He wanted to get back to Dad.

"Oh, all right." Alicia padded out of the water and put her shoes and socks back on, and they climbed up to the path.

A teenage boy trudged toward them. His shoulders slumped and his head drooped. Micah studied him carefully. "John?"

The boy's head came up, and he smiled. "Why, yes." John had grown taller and his voice was deeper.

"Remember us?" said Alicia. "We met you near the castle with your brother and friend."

"Of course," said John. "Wasn't it Micah and Alicia? You're the ones with the fairy tablet."

Micah shrugged his shoulders. "It isn't a fairy tablet. It's a . . ." He was going to say phone, but he caught himself. "It's an invention that lets us travel to the past."

"You left us so suddenly that day—like you vanished into thin air," said John. "You're still the same age. But that was over three years ago."

"I know," said Micah. "That's how it is. You grow older, but we don't."

"I still don't understand your invention. How does it work?" asked John.

"I don't really know," said Micah. "All I have to do is push PAST and type a name, and I go there."

"Did you put in my name?" asked John.

"We did," said Alicia.

"Why?" asked John.

"Uh, well, uh," said Micah. What could he say? He couldn't tell John he would be a prophet of God one day. He smiled. "We wanted to see green, beautiful England."

Alicia rolled her eyes. "Full-of-Yourself," she mumbled.

"This is a pretty place," said John. "But why me? I'm just a boy trying to do God's will."

Micah's neck muscles tightened. He looked at Alicia and widened his eyes for help.

Alicia smiled. "We live in America."

"America," said John. "I really want to go there. In fact, I have a strong impression I will go there one day and preach the gospel."[1]

Micah smiled. Relief washed over him. He would remember to thank Alicia later for changing the subject. "How do you know you'll go to America?"

"I just have a powerful feeling," said John.

"Someday you will . . . " said Alicia.

Micah put his finger to his lips, and she shut her mouth. He knew she was going to say John *would* go there and preach the gospel. "America is great. We love it there."

John pulled a small pocket watch from his vest. "I have to go back to work. Would you like to accompany me?"

Alicia giggled. "You speak in big words."

John smiled. "You have a funny accent."

"No, you have the accent." She laughed.

"I don't know how you got here or why you came to me," said John, "but it's nice to have your company."

They walked toward town.

"What were you doing out here?" asked Micah.

"I love to come to the woods to pray for God to guide me," said John. "I asked some of the boys from our church to have a prayer meeting in the hills with me every day after lunch. They came a few times, but then they stopped, so I'm feeling a little discouraged."[2]

"We'd love to have prayer with you," said Alicia. "In fact, we need to pray to get home."

"Wonderful," said John. "Let's stop in that grove of trees over there."

The three of them knelt in the crunchy leaves under the trees. Micah patted the soft cushion of dried foliage around his knees. He and Alicia were praying with a young prophet of God even before John knew he would be a prophet. Micah felt a chill tingle through him.

"Sometimes," said John, "I hear heavenly music in my head—like choirs of angels singing to me, and I know God is leading me."[3]

"That's wonderful," said Alicia. "God *is* leading you. I want Heavenly Father to lead me."

John smiled at her. "It's nice to have someone to pray with."

"I don't hear heavenly music," said Alicia. "So, I guess I need to try to feel the Spirit a little more when I pray."

"I don't hear music in my head either," said Micah, "but maybe if I hum some of my favorite church songs before I pray, it will help me be more spiritual."

"I'll pray," said John, "and ask God to take you home."

"Thanks," said Micah and Alicia at the same time. They looked at each other and smiled.

John prayed that all three of them would be kind to others and stay strong in their faith. John also asked Heavenly Father to help Micah and Alicia get home.

After the prayer, Micah waited for the peaceful feeling to come that they would get home right away. He remembered the joy he felt in the St. George Temple dedication with Brigham Young, knowing they would get back to their day.

The feeling didn't come this time. *Isn't God listening?* wondered Micah. He said a silent prayer for God to bless them. They needed to get back to Dad. *Tell me what to do, Heavenly Father,* pleaded Micah.

They stood and walked toward the town.

"So if you hear angels singing," said Alicia, "have you ever seen one?"

"Yes," said John. "I don't know if it was a dream or a vision, but I saw an angel flying through the heavens with a trumpet in his mouth, sending a message to all the earth."[4]

Micah glanced quickly at Alicia and smiled. "Angel Moroni," he mouthed.

Alicia nodded.

They approached the town. "Do you want to come and see my work?" asked John. "I'm using a lathe to make a set of chairs to go with a dining room table."[5]

"What's a lathe?" asked Alicia.

"It holds the wood steady and turns it while I cut and smooth the piece into a table leg or a chair leg."

"We'd love to see your woodwork," said Micah, "but I really want to get us back home. Our dad is waiting for us."

"I understand," said John. "It was very nice to see you again, and I wish you well in America."

"Thanks," said Alicia.

They waved good-bye to John and walked into a field. Micah pulled the phone out of his pocket and pushed PRESENT.

TEXT YOUR JOURNALS HOME, the phone said.

JOHN TAYLOR AND THE MYSTERY PUZZLE

"Oh," said Micah. "I wish it would just take us home."

"It doesn't seem to want to do that," said Alicia. "Pushing the PRESENT button isn't working this time."

"I wonder what Dad did to reprogram the phone," said Alicia.

Micah texted:

PRAYED WITH A PROPHET. MUSIC HELPS ME FEEL THE SPIRIT. JOHN KNOWS HE'S COMING TO AMERICA. PRAYED TO GET HOME. IS HEAVENLY FATHER LISTENING? WILL HE ANSWER MY PRAYERS?

He pushed SEND.

Alicia wrote:

JOHN LIKES TO PRAY. SO DO I. HE LISTENS TO HEAVENLY FATHER. I WILL TRY TO LISTEN TO WHAT HEAVENLY FATHER TELLS ME.

She sent it.

Micah pressed the PRESENT button. A wheel, divided into four sections with a center circle, appeared on the screen. Above it read:

SCRIPTURE PICTURE
COMPLETE FOUR SECTIONS AND THE
CENTER KEY

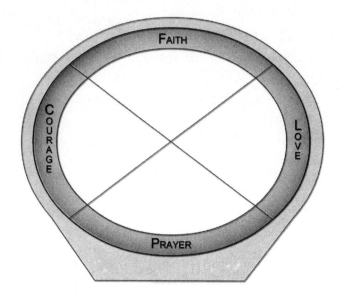

"What?" said Micah, putting his hand on his hip and stomping his foot on the ground. "Now we'll never get home!"

"Maybe it won't be a problem," said Alicia. "It might be a kind of fun puzzle." She looked at the phone again. "What's a scripture picture?"

"I'll bet Dad just put this on the phone," said Micah. "You know he loves making riddles and games like this."

The phone lit up: JOHN TAYLOR LOVES TO PRAY. D&C 10:5.

"Let me look the scripture up," said Alicia.

"No, I better do it."

"Why?" asked Alicia.

Micah thought for a minute. "Uh, I don't know. No reason." He felt frustrated. He wasn't getting them home like he planned. *I need to keep things under control by doing it myself*, he thought. He took a deep breath. *That's silly!*

Alicia can use the phone as well as I can. Besides I need to start being more considerate of her.

He handed the phone to Alicia.

"Thanks." Alicia pulled the scriptures up on the phone and scrolled to the Doctrine and Covenants. "Let's see, 10:5. It says 'Pray always.' So we need a picture of praying?"

"I guess," said Micah. "Let's go back to the woods where we prayed with John, and I'll take a picture of you praying."

"No, let me take a picture of you praying," said Alicia.

"All right," said Micah.

They walked back, and Micah knelt while Alicia snapped the picture. The photo appeared in a section of

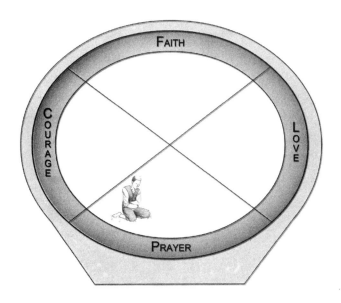

the wheel with "Prayer" printed below it.

FUTURE EVENTS lit the screen.

"There's no PRESENT button," said Alicia. "You look." She handed Micah the phone.

"It's not there. Oh well, there's no use arguing with the phone" He swiped FUTURE EVENTS.

JOHN EXPLORES ANCIENT RUINS OF KING ARTHUR

"I'd like to go there," said Micah, "but that's probably not going to get us home."

JOHN READS SHAKESPEARE AND SIR WALTER SCOTT.

"Wow, he's smart," said Alicia.

JOINED THE METHODIST CHURCH.

BECAME A METHODIST MINISTER AT AGE 17.

"No kidding, that's young to be a minister," said Micah.

BEGAN FURNITURE-MAKING BUSINESS IN HALE, HIS HOMETOWN.

LEAVES FOR CANADA.

"That's the one," said Alicia. "Let's go with him to Canada. I think that's where he joined the Church. Maybe that will help us get home."

They swirled into grayness, tumbling through space.

3

SAILING TO AMERICA

ALICIA crashed through dark thunder clouds and floated down near the back of a brick building. Micah landed beside her. They made their way around to the front where they could see a dock with a ship about to set sail. Sailors scurried across the deck, loading bags and crates. People clustered near the gangplank, waiting to board.

A gust of wind swirled Alicia's hair into a tangle. She brushed it off her face, but an updraft puffed it back into her eyes again. She flipped her head and turned into the wind so it would blow her hair back. Looking around, she spotted John, heaving a trunk onto the wooden walkway and shoving it up toward the ship's deck. She hurried over to him. "Hi, John," she said.

John glanced up. "Oh, hello, Alicia, isn't it? You're still young like you were a few years ago."

"Hello," said Micah, shaking John's hand. "Yeah, we are young. It's how the magic tablet works."

"I can't understand it," said John.

"I know," said Micah. "Neither can we."

Alicia looked up at John, feeling self-conscious. John was a man now, and she was still a child. "Want some help?"

"Sure," said John. "This is heavy. I wish I were like those sailors who can lift a trunk onto their shoulders and carry it aboard."

Dark clouds rumbled across the sky and lightning lit the horizon.

Alicia couldn't lift the chest, but she could help shove it up the gangplank. She pushed it over the rough boards with Micah and John beside her.

The three of them jostled the weighty trunk on to the deck.

"Thanks," said John.

"Can we come with you?" asked Alicia.

"Of course," said John.

Rain swirled into their faces.

Men removed the gangplank, and a dock worker unhooked the large rope that held the ship to the shore. He tossed it toward one of the ship's crewmen, who caught it and curled it into a circular pile on the deck. "Safe journey!" he called.

The crowd waved farewell, hunched against the moisture.

"Are you going to America?" asked Alicia.

"Yes," said John. "This has been my dream for a long time. I am sure God wants me to preach the gospel there."[1]

"And you will," said Alicia. *Oh no*, she thought and covered her mouth with her hands.

"What?" asked John.

"Uh, oh, nothing," said Alicia. She had to watch herself. She couldn't tell John he would join the Church and become the prophet.

"Where's the rest of your family?" asked Micah. "Are you alone?"

"My father took everyone to Canada two years ago," said John. "I stayed behind to finish up some of my family business."[2]

Lightning slashed the sky, and thunder rumbled behind it. The wind whipped rain at them. The ship continued out into the dark ocean. Would it be swallowed by the big waves? Alicia shivered. Her long dress wasn't much protection against the storm. Micah had on a jacket, and she wished he would let her wear it. But he didn't seem to notice.

The ship rose and fell with the waves. Alicia felt green inside. Would she be sick? She swallowed hard and breathed in the salty air.

Lightning hit the water not far away, and thunder rumbled from the depths of the ocean. Alicia could see a small fishing boat in the distance. The mast cracked in the wind and crashed onto the bow. The sailors scrambled for their oars and began to row for shore, paddling furiously.

"Look!" called a sailor from the other side of the ship. "A ship going down. Men overboard!"

Alicia turned to see the gaping jaws of the ocean swallow up the last of a sinking ship. Several sailors clung to the floating remains. One of the crew on John's ship threw a rope into the choppy ocean waves. The nearest man grasped it, and the sailor pulled him aboard. He lay dripping wet in a crumpled heap on the deck. The sailor cast the rope again and dragged another man to the ship. One more was saved, but the last man sank into the depths of the sea.

Drowned. Alicia shuddered against the thought. *He's dead.* Her stomach churned. She breathed deeply, trying to get thoughts about death and her sea sickness to go away. "Maybe the ship had better turn back."

Micah put his arm around her. "This is scary."

The wind tore at their clothes. Lightning crackled again. Cold rain pelted them.

John stood close, tall and straight, facing the storm.

"Aren't you afraid?" asked Alicia.

John smiled down at her. "I feel as calm as though I were sitting in the parlor at home. I believe I will reach America and perform my work."[3]

How would I feel, wondered Alicia, *if I were so sure of what Heavenly Father wanted me to do?* She knew God would keep the ship safe because John was on it, and he had to get to America to hear about the Church. Was Alicia that sure of what the Lord wanted her to do? She didn't know.

Giant waves loomed near the ship, one after another, ready to dash them into the sea. A swell, bigger than the rest, rose up in front of them.

"Hang on!" yelled Alicia. "That wave is going to get us!"

Water slashed across the deck, engulfing Alicia. She tried to grip the railing, but the water pulled her hands away. She gasped for air and choked. *Oh, no! I'm drowning,* she thought. The wave slammed her across the deck. Her head cracked hard against the cabin wall before the water rushed back into the sea.

Micah knelt beside her and grabbed her shoulders, pulling her to him. "Are you okay?"

She blinked the water from her eyes. "I don't know."

"We've got to get out of here," said Micah. "I don't want to lose you."

"I don't want to get lost," she said, gripping Micah's arm and struggling to stand. "Thanks for helping me. I'm glad you're here."

John hurried to her side. "Let's get you below and dry you off."

"I-I think we'll leave this storm and go somewhere else," said Micah.

Alicia smiled weakly. "Maybe we'll see you again." She felt grateful for Micah's thoughtfulness.

Micah pulled the phone from his pocket. "You've got to take us right now," he said to the phone.

Alicia shivered just as another giant wave loomed above them, ready to crash the deck again. Hurry, she thought. Reaching over Micah's arm, she pushed PRESENT, and they swirled into darkness.

"Safe journey," John called after them.

4

TAR AND FEATHERS

THE frosty ground crunched under Micah's stiff leather shoes. He shivered and buttoned his light jacket over his scratchy long-sleeved wool shirt.

Gray clouds blanketed the sky. A muddy road wound toward a town in the distance. Micah could see mostly log cabins and a few barns. Hills rolled past the horizon just like the ocean they'd just come from.

"How did we get to leave without texting?" asked Alicia.

"We can thank the phone for getting us out of a dangerous situation," said Micah.

YOU'RE WELCOME.

Alicia giggled. "The phone's listening to us."

"And talking to us," said Micah, holding the phone up. "Thanks again."

I'M SMILING. ☺

"I like talking to the phone," said Alicia. "Dad really fixed this phone so it's cool!"

Micah looked around again. "We don't know where

we are. The trouble with just pushing the PRESENT button is that we don't choose the place we go."

"Well, I really don't care where we are," said Alicia, pulling her homemade sweater snug around her. "I'm glad we got out of there, and I don't want to do any more sailing to America. That was scary."

"I know," said Micah, glad he was dry. "I wonder if any of our great-grandparents had to come across the ocean like that. What kind of storms did they have?"

"We should ask Mom and Dad, *if* we ever get home again," said Alicia.

Guilt settled in Micah's stomach. They were stuck in the past again, and it was his fault.

A light breeze chilled the air. "It's got to be the middle of winter," Micah said.

"I know we wanted to get out of the heat at home, but we've gone from a drenching storm to freezing cold weather," said Alicia. "Didn't John ever do anything in decent weather?"

"At least your long dress covers your legs," said Micah, looking down at his knee-length pants and long stockings.

"Yes, but not as good as my jeans. I'm still cold," said Alicia.

Micah watched her teeth chatter. Maybe he should give her his jacket, but he was cold too. He'd think about it—maybe later. His hands felt numb, so he jammed the one not holding the phone into his pocket.

The phone lit up: TEXT YOUR JOURNALS HOME.

Micah typed:

PIONEERS HAD A HARD TIME CROSSING THE OCEAN.

STORMS ARE SCARY. JOHN IS FAITHFUL. HE KNOWS GOD
WILL PROTECT HIM . . . DO I KNOW IF GOD WILL PROTECT
ME?

He pushed SEND and handed the phone to Alicia.
Alicia wrote:

FRIGHTENED BY STORM. ALMOST DROWNED. MICAH
SAVED ME. GOD SAVED JOHN. MAYBE GOD SAVED BOTH OF
US . . . DO I HAVE ENOUGH FAITH?

Micah took the phone back and pressed the PRESENT
button. The wheel, divided into four sections with a
center circle, appeared on the screen again.

SCRIPTURE PICTURE
COMPLETE FOUR SECTIONS AND
THE CENTER KEY

Micah rolled his eyes.

Alicia looked up at him. "This would be fun if I
wasn't so cold," she said through chattering teeth.

The phone lit up: JOHN TAYLOR HAS FAITH,
1 NEPHI 3:7.

"We already know that scripture," said Alicia.
"That's where Nephi says he 'will go and do the things
the Lord commands.'"

Micah pulled the scriptures up on the phone anyway
and scanned to the Book of Mormon. He scrolled to 1
Nephi 3:7. "I will go and do the things which the Lord
hath commanded, for I know that the Lord giveth no
commandments unto the children of men, *save* he shall
prepare a way for them."

"So how do we get a picture of that?" asked Alicia.

Micah smiled and cocked his head.

"Oh, no," said Alicia. "Do *not* go back to the ship to get a picture of John on the deck and me being slammed across it by the wave."

"Maybe the phone will let us use the drawing program to create our own picture of John standing strong in the storm."

YES appeared on the screen.

"Oh, my gosh!" said Alicia. "It hears and thinks. Dad really did fix this phone. It's so awesome! And Micah you're a genius for the drawing idea."

"Well," said Micah. "This is a twist. You've *never* called me a genius before. I guess I *am* pretty smart."

Alicia rolled her eyes.

"Well, I am," said Micah.

"Whatever," Alicia said. "Sorry I said anything." She took the phone, clicked into the program, and began to draw. Soon she had a picture of John standing tall in the storm on the ship. "Look, I put a lot of swirls in the wind, and see the big wave that's going to crash over the boat?"

"Good job," said Micah.

The drawing with "Faith" clicked into the grid next to "Prayer."

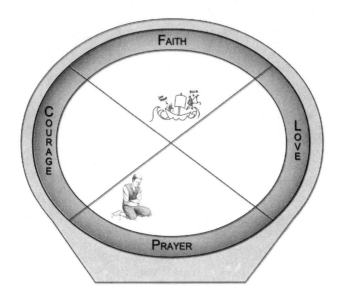

"Two down and two to go," said Micah, feeling really relieved. "Now, where are we?" he asked the phone.

NEAR COLUMBUS, OHIO, WINTER 1837.

The wind blew. Light snowflakes fluttered down on them. One landed on Micah's nose. He wiped it off and shivered again. Dark clouds clustered near the snowy earth at the edge of the rolling hills. A buggy drove up, and people began to gather.

"Swipe the PAST button," said Alicia. "I want to read what happened to John before this."

"I don't know if that'll work." Micah stroked the PAST button anyway. To his surprise, the screen started scrolling through past events.

LANDED IN NEW YORK, TRAVELED TO TORONTO, CANADA.

BECAME A METHODIST MINISTER.

MARRIED LEONORA CANNON.

LOOKED FOR A CHURCH WITH APOSTLES AND PROPHETS LIKE CHRIST HAD.

"That's just like Brigham Young," said Micah.

JOINED THE MORMON CHURCH, MAY 9, 1836.[1]

MET THE PROPHET JOSEPH SMITH IN KIRTLAND, OHIO.

"Oh, I wish we could have seen that," said Alicia. "I loved seeing the Prophet Joseph Smith meet Brigham."

People began to gather from the small houses that dotted the landscape in the distance. They drove carriages and buggies, clogging the road with horses and vehicles. Some of them sat in their wagons. Others found places to sit on the hillside. Micah dragged a log for him and Alicia to sit on. Others brought bricks and chairs.

"I guess this is near Columbus, Ohio, and John will be here," said Micah.

"I just heard that lady over there say there's going to be a preacher coming, and his name is John Taylor."

"Good," said Micah. "But if John's going to preach, why don't they meet in a church where there's some heat?"

"I don't know," said Alicia. "I'd like to be where it's warm instead of out here, sitting on the frozen ground of a small hill. This is not my idea of fun."

They waited in the cold.

Alicia turned to Micah. "Thanks for dragging this log over to sit on." Her teeth still rattled in the chilly air. She wished for her warm coat.

Alicia scanned the group, looking for John.

A buggy pulled up to the side of the hill, and John climbed down. He held his hand out for the lady sitting beside him and helped her step down.

"That must be Leonora," said Alicia. "She's pretty. Come on, Micah. Let's go say 'hi.'" Alicia ran toward them. "John, it's us."

"Micah, Alicia, how nice to see you. Glad you made it out of the storm." John shook their hands. "This is my wife, Leonora. Micah and Alicia are friends of mine."

"How do you do?" said Alicia, clutching her arms to her chest to keep warm.

"Hello," said Leonora.

"You're cold," said John. "Let me get the extra lap robes I have in the buggy. You can wrap them around you."

John draped a fur robe around Alicia's shoulders and handed a small quilt to Micah.

"Thanks," said Alicia. "I was getting very cold." John's kindness made her smile, and the fur robe felt so warm.

Alicia's eye caught a beautiful pin on Leonora's coat. "I like your flower pin." Alicia touched it. She didn't know if it was made of real diamonds or not, but it sure was pretty.

"Thank you," said Leonora. "The wife of Lord Aylmer, Governor General of Canada, gave it to me."

"Oh," said Alicia, "you must be a fancy lady."

Leonora laughed. "I am anything but fancy, but I was her companion for a while, and she was a fancy lady."

"Well, you look very pretty."

"Why are you preaching out here in the cold?" Micah asked John.

"The townspeople have asked me to speak, and sometimes they meet outside," said John. "But before I begin, let me find you a place to sit."

"We have an old log," said Micah. "All three of us can sit there."

"Fine," said John. "Thanks, Micah."

Micah smiled.

One of the men shook John's hand. "Thanks for coming to preach."

"In veneration for my Savior, I'm happy to speak," said John.

"You're using your big words again," said Alicia to John.

John raised his eyebrows and winked at her. "I said, 'I love my Savior.'"

Some men came running up to John's side. "Elder Taylor, Elder Taylor," said one of the men. "I have heard rumors that there are those who want to tar and feather you."

"Shhhhh," said John. "Talk more quietly."

The men continued in a whisper.

"What does 'tar and feather' mean?" Alicia asked Leonora.

"Mobs of angry men rip a man's clothes off and pour hot tar all over his body and then dump feathers onto the sticky tar." Leonora shuddered and hugged herself.

Alicia knew she was upset.

Leonora frowned and rubbed her hands together. "Sister Emma told how Joseph Smith was tarred and feathered one night. It was awful. The tar burned his skin, and they spent all night getting it off."

"I wouldn't want that done to me," said Micah.

"How terrible," said Alicia. "Why do mobs do that?"

"They do it to make a man stop doing whatever he is doing," said Leonora.

"Like preaching?" asked Alicia.

"Like preaching," Leonora said. "They probably want John to quit."

"Why don't they just stay home," said Alicia. "They don't have to come and listen."

"That would be a good idea," said Leonora.

"Why are some people mean to the Mormons?" asked Alicia.

"I don't know," said Leonora. "Probably for the same reason they're not nice to those of different races and religions. Sometimes people are afraid of others who don't think and behave like they do."

I hope I'm not like that, thought Alicia. *My friends and I are not all the same, and I like it that way.*

Alicia listened again to the men talking to John. "You can't preach. We're not strong enough to protect you. You'll be tarred and there's nothing we can do about it."

"Do you think the men will hurt us?" asked Micah.

"I pray to God they won't," said Leonora. "Let's have faith that we'll all be safe."

John looked at the men. "Heavenly Father wants me to preach, so I will. I don't know what will happen to me, but I don't want to pass up an opportunity to share my testimony of the gospel."

"But I saw the buckets of tar," said another man.

Alicia looked around. She thought she could smell the stink of tar, like when men fixed the roads at home.

"Trust in God." John patted the man's shoulder. "Trust in God."

"Oh," said Micah. "That takes a lot of courage."

"I know," said Leonora. "John is very valiant when it comes to teaching about Christ. Some call him 'Defender of the Faith.'" She looked down and twisted her shoe in the crusty snow. "I'm trying to be courageous like John."

Alicia wondered how strong her own faith was. What would she do if she could smell buckets of stinking tar waiting to be sloshed over her? She quivered at the thought.

John walked to the bottom of the hill, where everyone could see him. His brown hair was parted on the side and curled down over his ears. His face was clean-shaven except for the short beard he grew at the bottom of his chin. Beneath his black suit and matching vest, he wore a white shirt with a lace collar and a black bow tie.[2]

"John always looks very stylish," said Alicia to Leonora.

"He doesn't always look that way," said Leonora. "But when he is out in public to preach, he likes to dress up."

"I know he likes his shirt tucked in," said Micah. "I guess his parents taught him to dress well."

They climbed the rise to the log Micah had found and sat down.

"John's standing tall, just like he did on the ship," Alicia said to Micah.

"Trade me places so Leonora can't see what I'm doing," whispered Micah. "I'm going to snap a photo of John for the scripture picture."

Alicia shifted to the middle of the log, and Micah pulled the phone from his pocket.

John began to speak, "Gentlemen, I know your forefathers fought for the freedom of all men in this country during the American Revolution. Many of them died for our freedom." John paused, and then his voice rose in strength. "I understand you plan to tar and feather me for preaching. Is this the reason your father's died in that great war—so you would have the right to tar and feather someone?"

John stepped forward. "Come on with your tar and feathers, gentlemen. I am ready."

A hush came over the people, and every eye was on John.

John grabbed hold of his vest and shirt and ripped them open, ready for the tar and feathers.

Alicia watched the buttons pop off and fall onto the ground as Micah clicked the picture.

Everyone stood very still. They didn't move or say a word. Alicia clamped her hands together in front of her body. She felt the Holy Ghost fall upon the audience and knew John was a prophet of God even though he didn't know it yet.

John began to preach about the truthfulness of the Bible and then the Book of Mormon. Finally he shared his testimony of the Prophet Joseph Smith.

At the edges of the crowd, several men carrying big wooden buckets slipped away quietly. *I hope that's the tar and feathers going home,* thought Alicia.

After his talk, many people told John how good his speech was. Alicia watched several people pat his shoulder and call him 'Defender of the Faith.' One by one, the villagers returned home, and there were no tar and feathers that night.[3]

"That was a good speech," said Micah to John. "Someday I want to have a testimony as strong as yours."

"Study, pray, and fulfill your priesthood responsibilities," said John, putting his arm around Micah, "and you will."

"Thanks," said Micah. "We'd better get going."

"It was nice to meet you, Leonora," said Alicia. "I think you *are* a fancy lady like the governor's wife."

Leonora laughed. "It was wonderful to meet you."

"Maybe we'll see you again," said Alicia.

Micah and Alicia sat under a tree, and John and Leonora drove away in their buggy.

Alicia pushed the PRESENT button, and the phone lit up: TEXT YOUR JOURNALS HOME.

Micah typed:

JOHN ALMOST GOT TARRED AND FEATHERED. HE HAD COURAGE TO PREACH ANYWAY. FREEDOM DOESN'T MEAN YOU HAVE THE RIGHT TO HURT OTHER PEOPLE. I WANT TO BE KIND TO OTHERS.

He pushed SEND.
Alicia wrote:

LEONORA IS A FANCY LADY. SHE WORE A BEAUTIFUL PIN. JOHN SPEAKS LIKE A PROPHET OF GOD. I FELT THE HOLY GHOST WHEN HE TALKED. JOHN ISN'T AFRAID TO STAND UP FOR THE CHURCH. I WANT TO BE BRAVE LIKE HE IS. I DON'T LIKE TAR AND FEATHERING. I CAN BE UNDERSTANDING OF PEOPLE WHO ARE DIFFERENT THAN ME.

Micah pressed the PRESENT button. The wheel and words lit up on the screen again.

JOHN TAYLOR HAD COURAGE, JOSHUA 24:15.

"Let me look up the scripture," said Alicia. She took the phone and scrolled to the Old Testament in the Bible and found Joshua 24:15, "Choose you this day whom ye will serve . . . but as for me and my house, we will serve the Lord."

"I already have the picture," said Micah to the phone.
GOOD WORK appeared on the screen.

"That phone listens to everything we say," said Alicia.

Micah pulled the picture back up on his phone, and it slid into the third section of the wheel with the word "Courage" next to it.

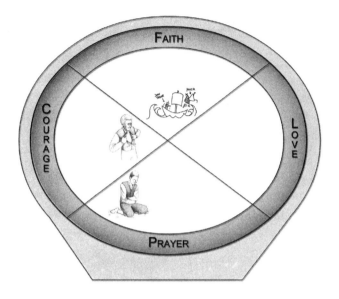

They both looked at the snapshot of John ripping his shirt open and the buttons popping off.

"Good action shot," said Alicia.

"We haven't finished the puzzle, so we can't get home," said Micah.

"Swipe FUTURE EVENTS then," said Alicia, "and let's see what happens next in John's life."

Micah swiped.

ORDAINED AN APOSTLE, DECEMBER 19, 1838.[4]

PUBLISHED THE *VOICE OF WARNING* IN NEW YORK CITY.

MISSION TO ENGLAND.

"I don't want to go on the ocean again," said Alicia.

PUBLISHED ARTICLES IN THE *MILLENNIAL STAR.*

EDITED NEWSPAPERS, *TIMES AND SEASONS* AND *NAUVOO NEIGHBOR.*

"That's four papers he wrote stories in," said Micah. "That's a lot."

DEATH OF THE PROPHET JOSEPH SMITH.

"Too sad and scary to watch," said Alicia.

JOHN TAYLOR, LIVING MARTYR

"I know he was shot," said Alicia. "I want to see if we can help him get well."

Micah pushed PRESENT, and darkness encircled them.

5

LIVING MARTYR

ICAH landed in the middle of a round, braided rug near a wooden rocking chair. Alicia dropped beside him. The phone lit up: JULY 1844, NAUVOO, ILLINOIS, JOHN TAYLOR HOME.

"Oops," said Alicia. "We landed in the middle of John's house. Look, the front door is open. Let's go outside and knock."

"It would be more polite," said Micah.

They scrambled off the floor and hurried to the front step. Micah turned to look back into the front room. A gentle afternoon breeze whisked past them into the house. A spinning wheel rested in the corner. Logs nestled in the fireplace, waiting for a chilly evening. A small table piled with papers and books stood at the far end of the room near a bed where John curled under a thin blanket, dozing.

Alicia knocked on the open door.

Leonora walked into the room. "Oh," she said. "Alicia and Micah! I'm surprised to see you. I didn't expect anyone, but I'm so glad you're here."

Micah smiled.

Leonora frowned. "You look as young as you did when I met you in Ohio, and that was several years ago."

"Oh, we do look young for our age," said Alicia, raising her eyebrows and looking at Micah.

"It's nice to see you again," said Micah, shaking her hand. *What do we do if she asks us why we haven't grown?* thought Micah. He breathed a prayer for help.

"That's beautiful jewelry you have on," said Alicia, pointing to a diamond pin Leonora wore.

"Thank you," sighed Micah without moving his lips.

"It's a watch," said Leonora, opening it for Alicia to see. "Oh, goodness, I didn't realize it was so late. I am to see Sister Emma Smith, Joseph's dear wife, this afternoon, and she's expecting me right now. She's having such a hard time since Brother Joseph was killed. But I hate to leave John alone. Could you stay?"

"We'd love to," said Micah, wiping his sweaty hands on his pants. *That was a close call*, he thought.

"I'll be off," said Leonora. "Thank you, children."

"Have a good visit," said John to Leonora. "Try to cheer Emma up a little. I know all of this has broken her heart."

"Oh, I thought you were asleep," said Leonora. "I'll see you later."

"Emma must be very lonely," said Micah.

"She is," said John. "We all miss Brother Joseph."

Leonora rushed from the house.

John stretched and yawned, pulling himself into a sitting position. "Micah and Alicia! Oh, it's good to see you."

Micah hung his head and twisted the toe of his shoe under the edge of the rug. He didn't know what to say.

John was still in bed and probably weak from being shot. How did you tell someone you were sorry they were almost killed?

Alicia ran to John and put her arms around his neck and hugged him close. "I'm so glad you're alive."

John held her close. "I am too."

"We almost got in trouble," said Alicia. "I was so afraid Leonora would ask us why we haven't grown up in the last few years. That's why I hurried and asked her about her pin."

John smiled. "If she asks me later, I'll smooth it over."

Alicia stood back and studied John. "You don't look good."

"Alicia," said Micah, "don't tell John he doesn't look good."

"Well, he doesn't," said Alicia.

John smiled. "It's fine, Micah. She's just saying what we all know. Even though it's been two weeks since I was shot, I'm in a lot of pain and still very tired."

Micah moved closer to the bed. John seemed okay to talk about things. "I want to know what happened the day the Prophet died. Do you mind telling about it?"

"No," said John. "I want you to know." He settled back onto his pillows. "But first I need a little something to eat. There are some peas and carrots in the icebox in the kitchen. Could you get me some?"

"I'll go," said Micah, wanting to be helpful like Alicia. *The icebox must be the fridge*, he thought.

"I would appreciate it," said John.

In the kitchen Micah saw the peas in a bowl on the table. At the end of the counter, he found a tin box about as big as the cooler they took to the beach. It felt cold to the touch. The fridge. He opened the door, and inside it was a slab of ice on a top ledge, dripping into a pan. The carrots sat on the bottom shelf next to a jug of milk. Excess water from the pan had leaked onto the carrots. He shook the water off. *This isn't like our big fridge with cold, filtered water and an ice maker,* thought Micah. He would remember to be thankful for his fridge when he said his prayers that night. He put the carrots and peas on a plate and carried them in for John.

"Thank you very much," John said, resting his head on a pillow. "Help yourselves to some." He motioned to the plate. "I'm trying to get better by eating my vegetables."

Micah and Alicia each took a few carrots and peas.

"The peas are so sweet," said Alicia. "I love them."

John sat up and took a carrot, but after a few minutes he laid back on the bed to rest, bending his left knee up and rubbing it. "Do you want to feel the bullet in my knee?"

Alicia shuddered. "Ewww, no."

"I'd like to," said Micah. "Are they going to take it out?"

"No, I'll leave the bullet in," said John. "I've had enough surgery."

Micah touched John's left knee lightly where he could see the red, swollen bump. "I don't want to hurt you."

"It still aches, but not as much as it used to," said John, "unless I bang my knee into something."

"Tell us about Carthage, please," said Micah.

John lay back on his pillows. "Some excommunicated

members who were angry with the Church published a newspaper called the *Nauvoo Expositor*. They printed stories about the Mormons that weren't true and said terrible things about our wives and children. We couldn't let them slander our families, so Joseph Smith and our Nauvoo City Council had the printing press destroyed."

"Why would the Prophet Joseph ruin a printing press?" asked Micah.

"Because he loved his family," said Alicia.

"Joseph and the City Council considered it a public nuisance and got rid of it," said John, rubbing the worry lines in his forehead. "Things are probably different now than in your time. It's fairly common here, if a town doesn't like something, to declare it a public nuisance and clear it out."

"It's not the same in our day," said Micah. "People let the police handle things, or they get lawyers."

John went on. "Folks in the surrounding towns were angry with the Mormons and wanted Joseph put in jail. Thomas Ford, the governor of Illinois, instructed Joseph to go to Carthage to tell the judge his side of the story. Joseph and Hyrum went to Carthage and asked Willard Richards and me to stay with them in the jail until the trial.[1] The rest of the twelve Apostles were in the east doing missionary work."[2]

John took a deep breath and coughed to clear his throat. Micah could tell it was probably hard for him to talk about what happened.

John continued, "The jailer in Carthage knew that Joseph and Hyrum were not criminals and they weren't dangerous, so he let us stay in an upstairs bedroom with a table and a bed, rather than in a locked jail cell."

Micah squeezed his eyes shut and took a deep breath, waiting for the sad story.

"Late in the afternoon of June 27, gloom hung in the air. We all knew something was about to happen. The Prophet had told us on the way to Carthage that he was going like a lamb to the slaughter."[3] John rubbed his feet together.

"Brother Hyrum asked me to sing 'A Poor Wayfaring Man of Grief' for him. I felt so depressed, I could hardly sing. But I took a deep breath and sang. When I finished, Hyrum asked me to sing it a second time."

John got a faraway look in his eyes, and a tear rolled down his cheek. He sighed and continued. "No sooner had I finished singing than I heard angry shouts outside and boots thumping up the stairs. We held the door shut, but the mob shot through the doorknob and smashed the door open. Men, faces blackened with axle grease, rushed into the room firing in every direction.

"I stood behind the door. When the men entered with their guns blazing, I knocked as many muskets down with my cane as I could, but the mob killed Hyrum. A bullet hit my left thigh. I ran for the window where another ball thumped my chest and threw me back into the room. It had shattered the glass in my pocket watch. Shots hit my left knee, left hip, and my hand. Oh, the pain I felt! And blood everywhere.

"I saw Joseph leap from the window, and shouts from the outside confirmed my worst fears—the Prophet Joseph, dead." Tears slipped from John's eyes, and he choked back a sob.

Micah could see that Alicia was crying too, and he had tears in his own eyes.

When John could speak again, he went on, "Our beloved prophet was gone. I didn't care that I was injured; I was just so sad about Joseph."

"How awful!" said Alicia. "The prophet was dead, and you were hurt."

"Shot five times," said Micah. "I'm glad Heavenly Father kept you alive."

"So am I." John pulled the sheet up to wipe his eyes. "When the mob saw Joseph dead, the men scattered, leaving the city. Brother Richards dragged me into the other room and put me in a jail cell and covered me with a dirty mattress to keep me safe in case the mob returned. Later a doctor gouged the bullet out of my hand with a penknife, and then others transported me to the Hamilton House Hotel a few blocks away. A doctor took the bullet out of my thigh and bandaged my hip."[4]

"Were you scared some of the mob would come back and kill you?" asked Micah.

"Yes," said John. "I only stayed there for a few days until I could travel. I'd lost so much blood from all my bullet wounds, I felt barely alive."

6

JOHN GETS WELL

"WHY did Heavenly Father let the mob kill Joseph and Hyrum?" asked Micah.

"Their work on the earth must have been finished," said John, "or the Lord would have protected them. And sometimes prophets seal their testimonies with their blood."

"What does that mean?" asked Alicia.

"That they die for the Church," said Micah.

"Maybe not just for the Church," said John, "but for their belief in Christ. Remember Christ's Apostles, Peter and Paul? They sealed their testimonies with their blood."[1]

"Oh," said Alicia. "I didn't know that. Why doesn't God stop people on the earth from being mean to each other?"

"That's a great question," said John. "We all have our agency. We can choose to be nice to others or to be hurtful. God isn't going to come down and stop us. But he knows our actions, and He will judge us accordingly."

"Big words again," said Alicia. "What does 'accordingly' mean?"

"If we are good, God will bless us, and if we are bad, he will punish us," said John.

"It would be very hard to judge everyone," said Micah.

"I know," said John. "We all have some good parts and some bad parts. That's why I'm so thankful for the Savior's Atonement so I can repent."

"How did you get back to Nauvoo?" asked Micah.

"I'll bet the bouncy wagon ride was very painful," said Alicia.

"I didn't ride in a wagon," said John. "It hurt too much. At first they tried carrying me on a litter, but that was torture."

"What's a litter?" asked Alicia.

"It's like a cot or a stretcher," said Micah. "I learned about them in Scouts."

"Well," said John. "Then they brought a sleigh pulled by a wagon and whisked me across the prairie grass to Nauvoo to be with my beloved family and friends."[2]

"Was Leonora with you?" asked Alicia.

"Yes," said John. "I was so glad to have her by my side."

Micah saw tears in John's eyes.

John continued. "At the time I told everyone, 'I shall never forget how grateful I felt toward my Heavenly Father. He has preserved me by a special act of mercy because I still have work to perform upon the earth.'"[3]

John turned himself and settled further into his pillows. "I'm weak from loss of blood, but I'm already healing."

"I'm so sad the Prophet Joseph is gone," said Micah.

"I am too," said John, taking a deep breath. "I have written something you might like to read about the

Prophet." He took a paper from the bedside table and handed it to Micah and Alicia.

Micah read: "To seal the testimony of this book and the Book of Mormon, we announce the martyrdom of Joseph Smith the Prophet, and Hyrum Smith the Patriarch. . . . Joseph . . . has done more, save Jesus only, for the salvation of men in this world, than any other man that ever lived in it. . . . In life [Joseph and Hyrum] were not divided, and in death they were not separated. . . . They lived for glory; they died for glory; and glory is their eternal reward."[4]

"That's beautiful," said Alicia. "I think the Holy Ghost inspires you in your writing—just like he told you what to say the day we heard you preach in Ohio."

This testimony of John's is part of the Doctrine and Covenants, thought Micah. He held the paper very carefully because it was an original copy of part of the Doctrine and Covenants. "These words will help everyone who reads them remember our love for the Prophet Joseph Smith."

"We do love him." John's voice cracked. "Yes, we do."

The door opened and shut. "Hello," came a voice.

"Leonora," said John. "We've had a good visit."

"I'm glad," said Leonora.

"We'd better be going," said Micah.

"We're praying for you to heal quickly," said Alicia. John caught her hand and squeezed it.

Micah gave him a hug and turned to Leonora, "Thanks for the peas and carrots. We loved them."

"You're welcome," said Leonora.

"Get well soon," said Micah, waving as they left the house.

They walked down Parley Street toward the Mississippi River. Shady trees lined the street. When they reached the water's edge, gentle waves lapped the shore.

"I know we want to get home," said Micah, "but I'm glad we came here. I'm feeling very thankful that John's still alive."

"I know Heavenly Father blessed him," said Alicia. "God wants him to become the prophet after Brigham Young."

"In those days, it was dangerous to be a member of the Church if there was a mob around," said Micah. "I'm thankful we live now."

"I know," said Alicia.

Micah pulled out the phone and turned it on. It lit up: TEXT YOUR JOURNALS HOME.

He typed:

JOHN GOT SHOT FIVE TIMES AND HE'S ALIVE. GOD PROTECTED HIM. WE TOOK CARE OF HIM FOR THE AFTERNOON. I'M GLAD I COULD HELP. I LOVE THE PROPHET JOSEPH SMITH.

He pushed SEND and handed the phone to Alicia.

Alicia wrote:

JOHN IS GETTING BETTER, BUT HE STILL LOOKS PALE. WE FED HIM VEGGIES. HE LOVES JOSEPH SMITH, AND SO DO I. LEONORA VISITED SISTER EMMA. SHE IS SAD THAT JOSEPH SMITH DIED. I AM TOO.

She hit SEND.

Micah took the phone back, pressed the PRESENT button, and the picture wheel appeared.

JOHN TAYLOR LOVED HIS FRIEND, THE PROPHET JOSEPH. JOHN 15:13.

"Let me look this one up," said Alicia.

Micah handed her the phone, and she scrolled to the New Testament in the Bible. She found the book of John and read, "Greater love hath no man than this, that a man lay down his life for his friends."

Micah couldn't swallow. He felt like crying. John had been willing to do what the Savior asked. He would have laid down his life for his friend, Joseph Smith.

Alicia looked up with tears in her eyes. "John has a lot of love, just like Jesus said."

"I know," said Micah. "I know."

"What about the picture?" asked Alicia.

"Oh," said Micah. "I forgot to take a picture."

"I want to make a drawing of the sleigh racing across the prairie grass," said Alicia.

"No," said Micah. "Let me draw the bullet in his knee."

HOW ABOUT BOTH, said the screen.

"That phone is a peacemaker." Alicia laughed.

They both finished their drawings on the screen and clicked them into the wheel with the word "Love."

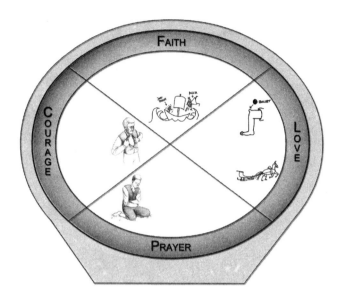

"Now what?" asked Alicia. "We need the center of the puzzle."

"Do we have to do that?" asked Micah. "I'll check." He pushed PRESENT.

PUZZLE INCOMPLETE, the phone said.

"So I guess we do have to do it," said Alicia.

FUTURE EVENTS lit the screen and Micah swiped.

WORKED ON THE NAUVOO TEMPLE.

TOOK HIS FAMILY WEST TO WINTER QUARTERS, NEBRASKA.

RETURNED FOR NAUVOO TEMPLE DEDICATION.

"I really want to see the dedication of the Nauvoo Temple," said Alicia.

"We're in Nauvoo," said Micah. "The center puzzle piece doesn't seem to be here."

"But we didn't see the dedication," said Alicia. "I

loved the St. George Temple dedication with Brigham Young, and I want to see the one here in Nauvoo."

"We have to keep going through his life," said Micah. "The center section is probably just before he dies."

"All right," said Alicia. "But I really want to see the dedication."

"Another time," said Micah. "We've got to get back home. Dad is probably flipping out, wondering what happened to us." Micah tried to listen to Alicia, but this time he knew he was right.

SECOND MISSION TO ENGLAND.

The low-battery light flickered in the corner of the screen and then flashed off.

"Oh, no," said Micah. "It looks like our two bars are almost gone." His stomach dropped to his knees. "We'd better find the middle circle of the puzzle and get home."

"What'll we do if the battery dies?" asked Alicia. "How'll we get home?"

Micah swiped FUTURE EVENTS AGAIN. "It's anybody's guess where we'll find the middle of the puzzle. We have to keep looking—and fast."

TREK WEST.

SETTLING IN SALT LAKE CITY.

"Maybe the center of the puzzle is a pioneer story," said Micah. He pushed PRESENT and darkness encircled them.

7

INDIAN FOOD

ALICIA landed next to a large sagebrush. Micah floated down smack on top of the bush near her. It crackled under his weight, spraying small twigs and tiny gray leaves everywhere. Alicia ducked her head and brushed the little leaves off her face. Some got in her mouth. "Yuck!" She spit.

The phone lit up: SALT LAKE VALLEY, 1847.

"I'll turn the phone off," said Micah, "to make the battery last longer." He held the green button until the phone went dark.

Alicia stood up and brushed herself off. The desert sand had a light crust on top of it that crumbled under her button-up shoes. Her dress this time had tiny blue checks on it.

"At least I don't have lace on my shirt," said Micah, rolling his eyes.

"And my dress doesn't have a high waist," said Alicia. "So I guess we're both happy."

"I know I am," said Micah, flicking the small sagebrush twigs from his long-sleeved tan shirt and brown pants.

Alicia looked around. Hills covered with red and yellow autumn colors surrounded this desert valley. Tall mountains stood guard in the distance.

"It must be fall time," said Alicia. She saw a man hammering boards on the side of a house. "I think that's John over there."

"He's finishing a wall," said Micah. "Maybe we can help him."

They hurried toward him.

"Alicia. Micah. How nice to see you! I am obliged to you for coming," said John with a big smile on his face.

"You always use big words." Alicia giggled.

"And you still have an accent." John chuckled.

"No, you do," said Alicia.

They laughed together, and he hugged her.

"I'm glad you're here, but it looks like you didn't get home after all. Is there some way I can help?"

"I wish," said Micah.

"I'll do anything I can for you," John said.

"We're okay," said Alicia, thinking of the puzzle. "We just have some things to find before we can get home." *If the battery doesn't go dead*, she thought.

John placed a hand on Micah's shoulder. "Well, if I can't help you, I could really use your assistance and Alicia's too. We just arrived in the valley, and you can see there's nothing here but desert. We need to get our houses built if we're going to survive the winter."

"What can I do?" asked Micah.

Alicia smiled. John's kindness seemed to be rubbing off on him.

"Will the two of you hold this board while I nail it to the studs?" asked John. "I can't afford to have a nail go in crooked. I only brought a small supply with me when I came west. It's a long way back to get more, so I have to make every one count."

"Sure," said Alicia. *Dad has a whole shelf in the garage filled with boxes of nails,* she thought. She would remember to tell Dad about John's building so they could be thankful for nails. There were so many things to be grateful for.

Alicia and Micah held, and John hammered.

John pointed to a stack of lumber. "Micah, would you get another board from that pile over there?"

Micah got a plank, and he and Alicia steadied it while John pounded the nails in. Micah carried the next piece of wood and held it for John. Soon the wall was finished.

"You are both good workers," said John. "It would have taken me all afternoon to do this alone."

"This is a piece of cake," said Alicia.

John looked around. "We don't have any cake here."

Alicia's hands flew to her mouth. "Sorry. That's just our way of saying it's easy."

"I guess we all have funny sayings," said John. "When I was a boy, our hired man used to say, 'We'll be done in two shakes of a lamb's tail.'"

Alicia laughed. "There's no cake and no lamb's tail here."

"But the wall looks great," said Micah.

Alicia glanced up to see three Indian braves on ponies riding toward them along with a pioneer man on horseback. They had baskets and sacks in their hands. "Oh, no, not Indians!"

"Indians are friendly," said John, smiling down at Alicia.

Feeling scared, Alicia moved closer to Micah. He put his arm around her and pulled her near. The braves and the pioneer man dismounted and walked up to John.

"Hello, George," said John. He turned to the Indians. "Greetings."

"Micah and Alicia, this is George Bean," said John. "He's a good friend of the Indians and can speak their language. These are Goshute braves."

They wore vests made from rabbit skins and long brown leather pants almost covering their moccasins. Each had black, matted shoulder-length hair.

"Hello," said Micah and Alicia together.

Alicia slid closer to Micah.

"These men come bearing gifts for you, Elder Taylor, because you saved the life of Yellow Bird," said Brother Bean. "Chief Little Face is very grateful you healed his son."

"God saved the boy's life, not me," said John. "So is the young Indian brave well?"

"After you and I blessed him a few days ago, he began to recover almost immediately. His measles are just about gone," said Brother Bean.

"That's wonderful," said John. "Is the tribe still at the hot springs?"

"Yes, but they'll be leaving in a few days," said Brother Bean.

The first brave stepped forward and opened his sack, pulling out moccasins and gloves. He bowed. "Many thanks."

"These are made of deerskin," said Brother Bean.

Alicia ran her hand across the brown gloves. "They're so soft."

"Your feet and hands will stay warm in these," said Micah.

"Thank you," said John.

The next brave gave John a basket filled with bulbs and roots. "Chief Little Face thanks you."

George pointed to the different bulbs. "These are sego lily bulbs and camas bulbs. Those roots are from the thistle."

"Are these all edible?" asked John.

"Yes," said Brother Bean.

"How do they taste?" asked Alicia. She tried not to make a face. *How gross*, she thought. *I want my French fries and hamburgers.*

"They're delicious," said Brother Bean, "and especially welcome since the pioneers don't have enough food for the coming winter. We wouldn't even know about any of these foods without the Indians."

The third Indian pulled a clay jar of honey out of a sack and two bags of nuts.

"Honey, pine nuts, and sunflower seeds," said Brother Bean.

"Now those I could eat," said Micah.

Me too, thought Alicia.

The last Indian handed John a small bag. He opened it and motioned for John to taste it.

John pinched some between his fingers. "It's meal of some kind." He took a small bite. "Delicious!" He passed the bag to Alicia and Micah.

Alicia tasted the meal. It was dark brown, sweet, and crunchy. "It's good."

"My family and I thank you very much," said John to the Indians. "I would like to find more of this food to feed my family in winter. Could you show us?"

Brother Bean spoke to the Indians in their language and then turned to John. "Saddle your horses, and we'll show you how to find the food yourself."

"Come," said John to Alicia and Micah. "You'd like to ride a horse, wouldn't you?"

"Sure," said Micah.

"I don't know," said Alicia. "I've never ridden a horse before. What if it bucks me off?"

"You'll be fine," said John. "I'll give you one of my gentlest ponies."

"All right," said Alicia. She sighed and wiped her sweaty hands down her dress. John led her to a small brown horse with a little saddle on its back.

John lifted her up.

Alicia's dress puffed out on either side of her. *This would be a lot easier in pants,* she thought. Nudging her toes into the stirrups made her feel more secure. She stroked the horse's neck downward. It felt smooth as silk.

"Hold the reins in your right hand like this," said John. "Lay the reins on her neck to the right if you want to turn that way, and to the left to turn the other way. But this pony will just follow the other horses so you won't even need to worry about guiding it."

John saddled the other horses and hooked several baskets onto the back of each. They rode with the Indians toward the hills until they came to a marshy meadow near the foothills where a mountain stream washed onto the grasslands.

The Indians talked to Brother Bean, and he

translated. "The camas plants grow in marshy areas like this, and the flowers resemble purple hyacinths."

"There," said Alicia, urging her pony toward a patch of lavender flowers.

"Let's take some home," said John.

They got off their horses and began to pull the plants up. The Indians showed them how to twist off the bulbs. With all of them working, they soon filled a basket.

I don't mind pulling these up, thought Alicia. *But I would not want to eat them.* She shuddered. *I'd love a peanut butter and jelly sandwich with a glass of milk right now—no pioneer food for me.*

When the basket was full, the Indians led them up into the hills where the ground was drier. Plants that looked like lilies grew in abundance. "These are sego lilies," said Brother Bean. "The braves say you can eat all of the plant, but the bulb is the most delicious." He pulled a small shovel from his saddle pack.

One of the Indians took it and began digging up sego lilies. Alicia looked at the dirty bulb. *That doesn't look delicious to me*, she thought.

"I'm so grateful," said John, looking at Brother Bean. "Please tell the braves that these plants will keep us from starving this winter."

Brother Bean and the Indians talked back and forth. The braves smiled and nodded their heads toward John.

"Where are the pine nuts?" asked Micah. "I like those."

"There are lots of pine nuts farther south," said Brother Bean, "but you can find some in these hills if you get them before the frost. Sunflowers grow in the meadows down in the valley."

"But what about the sweet meal?" asked John.

"Come with us," said Brother Bean. He led the way down the mountain. "Now we're going to a field where the wheat's been harvested. Only the dried stocks are left, but crickets are feeding on the wheat kernels that fell to the ground." Brother Bean found a dead pine branch on the way and broke off several sticks. "We need fire, and these dry pine needles will start quickly."

"I have matches," said John. He pulled some from his pocket.

Those matches must be precious too, thought Alicia, *just like the nails.*

When they reached the field, the Indians lit the pine and started a fire all around the edges. As the plants blazed toward the center of the field, hundreds of crickets jumped up out of the fire and fell back into it, burning to a crisp.

How gross is this? thought Alicia. The smoke blew in her face and made her cough. *Burned bugs in the smoldering field. This is not my idea of fun.*

When the fire died out, the Indians took their baskets and gathered the dead crickets. Micah helped them pick up the burned insects.

"Why are they gathering the dead crickets?" asked Alicia.

"Crickets are good to eat," said Brother Bean.

"Sounds gross to me," mumbled Alicia to herself. She should probably help, but she didn't want to gather dead bugs from the blackened ground. "You'd better take a snapshot of this," she whispered to Micah. "No one will believe it if you don't."

"I hope this is the center picture," Micah said.

Alicia looked at him. "I don't think the center of the puzzle will be burned crickets, but take the picture anyway."

"Maybe it will," said Micah.

"Guide your horse to the other side of me so the men won't see," said Alicia.

She watched Micah slip the phone from his pocket, turn it back on, and click the picture. He glanced around quickly and then shoved it back in his pants. Alicia breathed a sigh of relief. No one saw.

"In the village, the squaws grind the burned insects into meal and mix it with honey," said Brother Bean.

So this was how the sweet meal was made! Alicia raised her eyebrows and looked at Micah. "I think I'm gonna be sick," she whispered.

"Me too," said Micah.

John chuckled, and then his face turned serious. "When we are low on food this winter, the bulbs, nuts, and cricket meal will taste mighty fine."

"Yuck," said Alicia. "Double yuck." She didn't think she would ever be hungry enough to think this food was good. She wished for the cheesy pizza they had for dinner last Friday night.

After they picked up all the dead crickets, they turned their horses toward town. "Thanks for your help," said John. "We'll gather some more of these later for the winter."

The Indians and Brother Bean took the fork in the road toward the hot spring where the braves and their families camped.

"Thanks again," called John, waving.

Alicia, Micah, and John rode toward John's home.

Micah pulled the phone out of his pocket, turning it on. "The low-battery light flickered again."

Fear gripped Alicia's heart. What would they do if the battery went dead?

"What does that mean?" asked John, pointing to the phone.

"It means the magic tablet might stop working, and then we'll never get home," said Alicia.

"I'm going to try to get us home before the battery dies," said Micah.

Alicia took a big deep breath. She tried not to feel sorry for herself, but it wasn't working. "Thanks for taking us today," she said to John.

"Thank you for helping me," said John. "We got a whole day's work done in a few hours, plus food for the family."

With the others, Alicia rode her pony into the corral, swung her leg off the horse, and stepped on to the ground. John showed her how to undo the saddle cinch. She carried the saddle and blanket over and set it on the fence. *This is heavy*, she thought. John helped her unbuckle the bridle and take the bit out of the pony's mouth. Alicia hung it over a post.

"You're a good rider," said John.

"Thanks," said Alicia, giving John a hug. "Pray for us. I really want to get home."

"I will," said John.

"I don't know if prayers are going to help," said Micah. "I think we're done for this time. If the battery dies, there's nothing we can do."

John put his hand on Micah's shoulder and looked into his eyes. "Never give up your faith, my boy. If God wanted to turn a river from its course or level a mountain, He could."

"My faith isn't that strong," said Micah. "This trip is not going like I thought it would. First, we couldn't get home after seeing you as a boy. Now we have to finish a silly puzzle, and the battery is almost dead. How can I have faith? How will Heavenly Father help us through all these problems?"

"I don't know the answers," said John. "But trust the Lord. He will help you. And please come find me if the magic tablet doesn't take you home."

Alicia and Micah waved good-bye and walked into the desert. They sat near a giant sagebrush. Alicia could see sunflowers waving in the distance. A picture of mashed potatoes came into her mind. Her mother made them so creamy. She would be so grateful for food if they ever got home. "Please try to travel to Mom and Dad."

"I don't think I'll be able to," said Micah, looking at the phone.

LOW BATTERY flashed again. TEXT YOUR JOURNALS HOME lit up on the screen.

"Make it short," said Alicia, "to save the battery."

Micah typed:

HELPED BUILD A HOUSE, RODE A HORSE, MET SOME INDIANS. THEY SHOWED US HOW TO FIND FOOD THAT GROWS IN THE WILD. WE DIDN'T EVEN HAVE TO BUY

IT AT THE STORE. MY FAITH IS WEAK. HOW DO I GET
STRONGER FAITH?

He sent it.

"That wasn't short," said Alicia, taking the phone.
Worrying, she typed fast:

JOHN HEALED AN INDIAN BOY FROM THE MEASLES.
THE INDIANS BROUGHT JOHN GIFTS OF FOOD. JOHN WAS
THANKFUL BECAUSE HIS FAMILY WOULDN'T STARVE.
INDIAN FOOD IS GROSS. PLEASE TAKE ME HOME.

She hit SEND.

Micah pressed the PRESENT button, and the wheel
appeared on the screen.

JOHN LOVES OTHERS, D&C 88:123, the screen said.

"I'll find it," said Alicia.

Micah handed her the phone, and she pulled
the scriptures up and scrolled to the Doctrine and
Covenants 123:88. She read, "Love one another."

"I want to love everyone," said Alicia. "I'll especially
love this phone if it'll take us home."

NO HANDOUTS HERE, BUT YOU *CAN* SOLVE THE
PROBLEM, appeared on the phone.

Micah rolled his eyes. "We'll never get home."

Alicia sighed.

SCRIPTURE PICTURE ACCEPTED, the phone said. The
puzzle filled the screen, and the cricket picture appeared
in the "Love" space along with the sleigh and bullet in
John's knee.

"No," said Micah. "It's supposed to be the center
circle."

YOU HAVEN'T FOUND THE CENTER PICTURE YET, the
phone said.

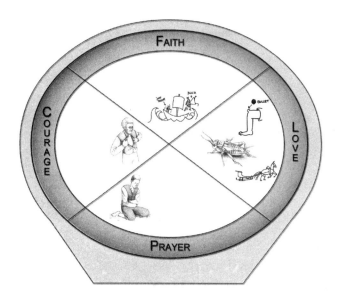

"What are we going to do now?" asked Alicia. "I don't want to live in this pioneer desert, but maybe we'll have to. I'm trying very hard not to feel sorry for myself." She wiped a tear from her eye.

LOW BATTERY flickered again.

WHAT A PAIR: ONE OF YOU HAS LITTLE FAITH AND THE OTHER FEELS SORRY FOR HERSELF. The phone buzzed and FUT . . . EV . . . N . . . flashed across the screen.

"Wait!" yelled Micah. "Where are we going?"

"Someplace else, obviously" muttered Alicia under her breath.

They faded into the darkness.

8

ESCAPE

MICAH landed on a white tile floor made up of hundreds of little hexagonal-shaped pieces laid out in a perfect pattern—an old fashioned kind of floor he'd seen in museums and train stations. A machine with paper stacked in it stood to the side of the room. Maybe it was an ancient printing press. He didn't know for sure.

He looked down at his clothes. He had on a dress! And a cape with flowers embroidered on it! Fluffy pants under his skirt and long stockings like Mother wore! They came down to shiny black shoes—like Alicia had for church on Sunday! Girl clothes! He looked like Little Bo Peep! He didn't care where he was, he wasn't wearing these things. He pulled at the cape but couldn't tell how to unhook it.

Alicia drifted down beside him and glanced at herself. "Look at this dress-up outfit—a lacy white top with a puffy skirt. I must have on a lot of frilly slips to make my dress stand out so much." She stood up and twirled around. Her skirt flared into a full circle.

Alicia's clothes are cute, thought Micah, *but I hate mine.* He peeked out the lace curtains that covered the window and saw a little boy running down the street, chasing a ball. A dog ran after him. He had on a dress and a cape too.

"Help me out of these clothes," said Micah. "I am *not* staying dressed like this."

Alicia laughed and reached for the button that fastened the cape around his neck. She undid it. "I wish I could take a picture. You'd never live it down."

"Not on your life," said Micah. "You're dead meat if you do. Besides, you can't—the phone's dead."

"Bonjour," said a man, hurrying into the room. *"D'où êtes-vous venus?"*

"What?" asked Micah.

"D'où êtes-vous venus?"

Now we're really in trouble, thought Micah. *I don't even know what this guy is saying.*

John rushed into the room with a suitcase in his hand. "I've got to catch the next train."

Oh no, thought Micah, *the phone's dead, so we can't get away from here. We need to go with John, but I'm not leaving this room in a girl dress.*

"John," said Alicia.

"Oh, goodness!" said John. "It's nice to see you two, but I can't greet you properly right now. What a time I'm having."

"I'm wearing a dress," said Micah, "and this man can't even speak English."

"Yes he can," said John. "This is Brother Decloux. I don't think he knew you spoke English."

"I didn't," said Brother Decloux. "I just asked where you came from."

"Oh," said Micah. "Will you help me find some boy's clothes?"

"Brother Decloux, these are my friends, Micah and Alicia," said John, dashing for the door.

"Bienvenue," said Brother Decloux. "Welcome."

No one is listening to me, thought Micah. *I need out of this dress.* He pulled at the cape and ripped it off his shoulders, throwing it on the floor.

"I'm in a real hurry to catch the train," said John. "The police want to arrest me for holding a conference here in Paris."

"Can we come with you?" asked Alicia.

"I'd love to have you," said John. "But we have to leave right now."

"I'm not going in a dress," said Micah again.

"We have loved having Elder Taylor with us," said Brother Decloux to Micah and Alicia. "He has been such a great missionary."

Micah watched John turn the handle and push the door open.

Brother Decloux went on, "Elder Taylor's had the Book of Mormon translated into French and begun a French newspaper, *The Star of Deseret.*"

"I have to go," said John to Brother Decloux.

Brother Decloux ignored John and went on. "He also arranged for the Book of Mormon to be translated into German and established a German newspaper, *Zion's Banner.* He has held conferences and debated many prominent ministers in the area."[1]

"Brother Decloux," said John, holding his hand up as if to stop more words from coming out of Brother Decloux's mouth. "You are a dear friend, and it's wonderful that you tell others about the Lord's work here, but I really must go. The police will be here any minute."

"*Évidemment.* Of course," said Brother Decloux.

A fist pounded on the front door. "*Ouvrir,* open up," came a shout from outside.

"It's the police," said John. "I don't want to go to jail." He grabbed his suitcase and raced out the door. "Come with me, Micah and Alicia—make haste!"

"I am not going in a dress," said Micah. *But I have no choice,* he thought. *I don't want John to go to prison.*

"The carriage is waiting," called John. "Pick up your cape, Micah."

Micah grabbed the cape and caught Alicia by the hand.

"It was nice to meet you, Brother Decloux," Alicia said as they followed John.

Micah heard Brother Decloux open the front door and say, "Come in, gentlemen. I understand you are looking for John Taylor. Let me tell you about him . . ."

John wrung his hands together as they climbed into the carriage. "I hope Brother Decloux can stall them until we're safely away."

Micah's heart pounded in his chest as they drove. He scanned the streets, looking for police. He didn't want to go to prison, and he didn't want John to either. Would Heavenly Father keep them safe? Things were getting worse, not better.

"I've got to get out of these clothes," said Micah.

"Stop already," said Alicia. "You've said that at least a hundred times."

John chuckled.

"This is nothing to laugh at," said Micah, "and I'm going to ask the phone why I'm dressed this way if we ever get the battery charged."

"There's no time to stop and buy you new clothes," said John. "Young boys wear dresses here in France. I'll admit you're a little old to be in that kind of an outfit, but littler boys wear them all the time. And they usually have their hair in long ringlets. You're lucky you don't have curls all over your head too."

"Ahhh," said Micah. "I'm not a *little* boy! What can I do?"

"Maybe this was the phone's idea of a joke," said Alicia.

Micah frowned. This was no joke to him.

The carriage pulled up to the train station bustling with travelers.

John pushed his way through the crowd. "Look, there are some street musicians." He pointed to a man playing a violin and a group of singers. "Some of them are in costume. One of the boys is about your size, and he's wearing pants. I'll ask him if he'd be willing to change clothes with you in the toilet."

"The toilet?" asked Micah.

"It's sort of an outhouse with just a hole in the floor, but it'll be enough room to change."

John talked to the young singer. The boy nodded his head.

"Whew," said Micah to Alicia. "It looks like he'll trade."

John steered Micah and the boy toward the toilet. "Alicia and I'll be at the ticket counter. John pointed in the opposite direction. Come find us when you're done. But hurry."

The toilet stunk worse than the barnyard at his grandparents'. Micah tried not to breathe as he skinned off his clothes and took the boy's white shirt and a black bow tie. The boy gave him a tight, black, fitted jacket that buttoned up the front and fitted long pants that almost covered his pointy black shoes. *Oh well. It's better than a dress,* thought Micah. *I never thought I'd be happy with shiny, pointed shoes.* He was grateful to the boy, but all he knew how to say was, *"Merci."*

The boy smiled down at his new clothes and ran back to the singers.

Micah jostled his way through the crowd to the ticket counter.

"Three for La Havre," John said, paying for the tickets.

"Feel better?" John asked him.

"Sort of," said Micah. He never would have chosen tight black pants or pointed shoes.

They walked toward the trains and found their track. "Climb aboard," he said.

"These are big steps," said Alicia, reaching her foot up to the tall wrought iron stairs.

"I'll help you up," said John, taking her hand.

They found two empty seats facing each other. Alicia and Micah sat on one side and John on the other.

John glanced around. "I hope the police haven't followed us. When word gets out that I'm gone, all the railways will be watched. I don't think we can cross the channel to England without being found. We'll have to stay out of sight for a few days."

"What'll we do?" asked Alicia. "Can we catch a boat at La Havre?"

"We can sail from there, but first I want to get in touch with the members of the Church and see if we can hold some secret conference meetings until the police have given up searching for me. Then we'll go to Jersey, a little island off the coast of England, to visit those members and then on to England itself."[2]

"Could we stay with you now?" asked Micah. "The black box isn't working anymore, and I don't know how we can get home. You may be stuck with us for the rest of your life."

"I'd love to have you as part of my descendancy," said John, winking at Alicia.

"There you go with your big words again," said Alicia.

"I don't think that's even a word," said John. "I just made it up so you'd remark on my big words." John laughed and put his arm around Alicia.

Alicia smiled, but Micah could tell she was worried. She didn't even laugh at John's joke.

"If we stay with you," said Alicia, "can we sail on a day that's not stormy?"

"You're remembering the trip to America," said John. "God protected us all."

"He really did," said Micah. *Maybe I do have a little faith*, he thought.

The train sped across the countryside, past fields and farms.

"I can smell the sea," said Alicia.

"You'll see it soon," said John.

As the train rounded the next bend, the ocean stretched clear to the sky. White caps ruffled the tops of the waves, and a breeze blew in the open train windows.

John glanced around again. "No police. We're almost to La Havre. We'll be safe there."

Micah's stomach felt like a lead ball. How would they ever get home? "Now that we're settled in," he said to John, "I think Alicia and I'll take a walk down to the sea shore. We need to pray about getting home." But how on earth could God help them? He wouldn't drop a new battery from heaven. Or would he?

"Prayer is a good idea," said John. "Use your faith."

"Maybe I have a little," said Micah.

"You do," said John. "Just like I have faith that someday the police won't chase missionaries when they preach; and the gospel will spread over all the earth, like the trumpeting messenger represented in my dream as a youth." [3]

Micah pictured the angel Moroni statue on top of temples all over the world.

"I want to have faith like you, John," said Alicia.

"Right now I'm concentrating on faith to get us home," said Micah.

He and Alicia walked down the path to the seashore. Micah's pointed shoes pinched his toes. *I hope I don't have to wear these narrow shoes permanently, but at least I'm thankful I don't have on that dress,* he thought.

The hills above the ocean boasted green grass and moss-covered rocky banks. The sun peeked out from a cloud, warming the day.

"Let's walk between the hills so we don't have to climb down the moss," said Alicia. "I want my white dress to stay clean."

Girls, thought Micah. *Who cares if you stay clean?*

They padded to the shore and pulled off their shoes and socks and carried them. Micah's suit still felt tight, but at least his feet were free. The sand squished between his toes. "I'm glad to get rid of these shoes." They came to a quiet spot between the sand dunes, and Micah stopped. "Let's kneel for prayer. Will you pray?"

"I want to have enough faith to help us figure out how to get home," said Alicia, folding her arms and bowing her head. As she prayed, Micah felt the lead in his stomach lighten.

"I hope Heavenly Father will show us to a way to recharge the phone battery," said Micah.

"He will," said Alicia. "He will."

They walked along the shore, washing their feet in the rising tide and popping seaweed bubbles with their toes along the way.

"This is fun," said Alicia, "but I'm not getting any ideas about how to get home."

In the distance they could see an old woman sitting on a rock not far from the water's edge. The dark color of her long dress blended into the stone cliff behind her. A dingy lace cap covered her head. Wisps of gray hair, aided by the sea breeze, brushed her wrinkly face. Micah watched her flashing something back and forth with her hands. "I wonder what's she's doing?"

Alicia walked a little faster toward the woman. "Look, she's beaming light on the rock."

"What?" asked Micah. "That's a strange thing to do."

When they got a little closer, Micah could see she had a fish resting on the rock. With a magnifying glass in her hand, she caught the sunlight and focused it onto the fish, leaving it just long enough for a bit of steam to rise from the fish. Then she flicked the light to another part of the fish.

"What are you doing?" Alicia asked the old woman.

"*Je ne comprends pas*," came the reply.

Alicia smiled and nodded at her.

"She probably doesn't understand English, and we don't understand French," said Micah.

The woman flashed the sunlight on to the fish over and over. As soon as a puff of steam rose, the woman moved the light ray to another spot. The air began to smell like grilled fish.

"I guess she's cooking the fish," said Micah. "The light probably gets hot when it's focused in a certain place."

"That's not going to help us," said Alicia.

"So all we've learned so far after praying about recharging a battery is how to cook fish with a magnifying glass on the seashore," said Micah. "It's not something I needed to know, and it won't get us home. But it's nice to understand that sunlight can be used for many things."

"But not batteries," said Alicia.

"Maybe . . ." said Micah. He had an idea.

"Maybe what?" asked Alicia.

"Sunlight can recharge a battery," said Micah.

"How do you know if this is that kind of battery?" asked Alicia.

"Well, Dad always lectures us about 'going green' with everything," said Micah. "Maybe the battery can be recharged with solar power."

"How can we tell?" asked Alicia.

"Let's look at the battery," said Micah. He pulled the phone from his pocket, turned it over and popped the battery out. "I don't know for sure, but maybe these small circles are solar cells."

"Well, it won't hurt to try to recharge it," said Alicia. "It isn't working now anyway, so we have nothing to lose."

"You're right," said Micah.

"But we don't have a magnifying glass, and there's no way to tell this lady what we want. We can't even explain the phone in English, so we for sure can't do it in French."

"Well, let's go find John and see if he can locate a glass for us."

They smiled at the woman and waved good-bye.

"*Au revoir,*" said Micah. "I think that means good-bye."

The woman smiled; her wrinkles raced upward to her twinkling eyes. "*Au revoir.*"

"She's nice," said Alicia. "I could be her friend."

BURNING GLASS

J OHN, John," called Micah. "I have an idea about the magic tablet, but I need your help."

"What can I do?" asked John.

"Well, the pho . . . uh, magic tablet needs power to work," said Micah. "We saw a woman down by the seashore cooking a fish with the rays of the sun."

"Micah thinks maybe we can use the sun to fix the magic tablet," said Alicia.

"I don't understand," said John. "I can't collect the sunlight for you."

"Oh!" Micah laughed. "I forgot to tell you that the lady had a magnifying glass she used to focus the rays of light onto the fish to cook it."

"Hmmm," said John. "What an idea. So you need me to see if I can find you a glass."

"Yes, please," said Micah.

"I think our landlady had a magnifying glass on her side table when I paid for our room," said John.

"I hope she'll let us use it," said Alicia.

"I hope so too," said John.

They followed John downstairs and stood behind

him while he knocked on the landlady's open door. A small woman with silver-white hair came toward them.

"*Bonjour*, Madame," said John, bowing slightly. "I came to ask a favor of you. Do you have a magnifying glass we could borrow for a few minutes?"

"For yourself?" asked the lady.

"*Non*, the children," said John, standing aside and putting his arm around Alicia.

"Children? *Non, non, non*," said the lady. "They are careless and will break it."

"*S'il vous plait*. Please," said John.

"*Non*," said the landlady. "I need it for reading." She shut the door.

"So much for that," said John.

"Now what do we do?" asked Micah.

"How about the old woman on the beach," said Alicia. "She's the one we got the idea from in the first place. But we can't talk to her."

"I can translate," said John. "I'll go with you."

"Hurry," said Alicia running ahead. "I hope she isn't gone."

The three of them jogged along the beach until they came to the rock where the woman had cooked her fish. No one was there. All that was left were fish bones scattered along the sand.

"Let's ask those children if they have seen her," said Micah, pointing to some boys playing ball.

John hurried over to them. "Have you seen an old woman?"

"*Oui, oui*," said one boy. He turned toward a cave in the rocky cliff.

Beyond sat the old woman mending a fish net.

"There she is." Alicia clasped her hands together and rushed toward the old lady. "Ask her, please."

"*Bonjour,*" said John, bowing slightly.

"*Bonjour,*" said the old woman.

"Do you have a magnifying glass the children could borrow?" asked John in French.

"Of course," replied the woman. She handed Alicia the glass.

"*Merci, merci,*" said John.

"*Merci,*" said Alicia.

Micah pulled the phone from his pocket and took off the back. He popped the battery out and laid it on the rock. "These small circles around the edge of the battery may be solar panels."

"I really hope so," said Alicia, holding the magnifying glass above the rock, tilting it until she caught the sun's rays. She focused the beam of light directly on the battery.

"Careful," said the old woman in French. "If you keep it there too long, it will get so hot it will make fire."[1]

John translated.

"I guess it could ruin the battery if it gets too hot," said Micah.

Alicia flicked the ray out to sea for a minute.

Micah touched the battery. It sizzled his skin. "Owww." He blew on his finger to get the pain to go away. "We can't use the magnifying glass. The heat from it will burn the battery."

"Okay," said Alicia. "But how do we recharge the battery?"

"Well, like we said, maybe there are tiny solar cells in

the battery that will just recharge if we set it in the sun."

"But it's probably not as fast as the magnifying glass," said Alicia. "How do we know how long it will take to charge?"

"Beats me," said Micah. "We'll leave it for the day and see what happens." He set the battery on the rock in the sun.

"This magnifying glass is fun," said Alicia. "Maybe it will burn up that spider." She watched a spider crawl along the sand. She focused the light on the spider, but it scuttled away. "How about a piece of seaweed?" Alicia turned the ray of light onto a seaweed bulb. The sun burned into it, and the bubble popped and fizzled into ashes in the sand. Alicia looked at the magnifying glass in her hand. "Burning glass."

Micah glanced around. What could they do for the rest of the day while they waited for the battery to recharge? Some boys played with an old rag ball down the beach, but they were younger than Micah.

John looked at him, guessing his thoughts. "The boys your age are working in the fields or out on the fishing boats."

Wow! thought Micah. *If I lived here I'd have a job. I'm glad I can still be with my friends and go to school.* He looked over at Alicia who was helping the old woman gather the fishing net.

She was talking to Alicia. John translated. "My old hands have a hard time tying the knots to mend the net."

"Maybe I can do it if you show me how," said Alicia.

Alicia is being her helpful self, thought Micah. "What can I do?" he asked.

"Micah, she'll show you how to tie the knots to mend the net too," said John. "Then help her gather it into a pile so it doesn't get tangled."

As they mended the net, Micah listened to John's words as he talked to the old woman. He couldn't understand what they said, but the words flowed like music. *French is cool*, he thought.

The sun hollowed itself a nest in the sea and was gone. Night settled over the beach. An old man came to the woman and gathered the mended net. They trudged toward the village.

Micah picked up the battery and snapped it into the back of the phone. The screen remained black. Micah's heart sunk. "I guess it didn't work."

But soon the LOW BATTERY light flickered on. "Woo hoo," said Alicia, raising her hands in the air. "At least it's working."

"Maybe if we charge it again tomorrow, it will be back to full power," said Micah.

Early the next morning, they brought the phone back to the rock and put the battery in the sun. The old woman walked their way with a string of four fish. When she reached them, she laid the fish on the rock and handed Micah the magnifying glass. She pointed to the fish.

"I think she wants me to cook our breakfast," he said.

Micah focused the beam of light from the glass onto the fish. As soon as it began to sizzle, he moved it. The smell of cooking fish made his stomach rumble. "This is a great way to cook, but I think a frying pan over a fire would be faster."

"You're probably right," said John, walking up behind them. "But wood for fires is expensive here, and sunlight is free."

Alicia took a turn cooking and soon the fish were done.

Micah let the small bites of white meat melt in his mouth. *At home I would have complained about the bones in the fish and taken big bites to hurry out and be with my friends. From now on I'll be grateful for the food Mom fixes.*

Micah and Alicia helped the old woman mend the nets again. John wandered down the beach to talk with people.

"He's probably telling them about the gospel," said Micah. "He's a great missionary."

The sun dipped into the ocean, and John returned to them.

Micah put the battery back in the phone.

It lit up. I'M BACK!

Micah felt humble. "I can't believe Heavenly Father blessed us like this."

"I knew He would," said Alicia.

Micah smiled at the old woman. "Thanks for the fish."

John translated.

"*Les enfants seront bénits pour leur fidélité,*" the woman said to John.

"What did she say?" asked Alicia.

"That you will be blessed for your faithfulness."

"How does she know?" asked Micah. *Maybe Heavenly Father is helping my faith grow through this stranger,* thought Micah.

"She is wise," said John. "Very wise."

88

She waved to the children. *"Au revoir."*

"Good-bye," Micah and Alicia said together.

The old woman walked into the mist gathering on the shore. The old man shuffled toward her. Soon they were gone.

Micah smiled. His faith was strong now, but would it last? Would he doubt again?

"Heavenly Father didn't answer in the way I thought he would," said Alicia.

"He didn't drop a new battery down from heaven," said Micah, remembering his thought.

"God usually helps us solve our own problems," said John.

Micah shook John's hand. "We're going to try to get home again. Thanks for everything."

Alicia gave John a hug. "I'll miss you. Thanks for your kindness."

John waved. "Come back if you need to." He crunched through the sand toward his room.

Micah turned the phone on.

It lit up: WELCOME BACK! TEXT YOUR JOURNALS HOME.

Now that the phone was back, Micah had to ask about the French clothes. "Are you the one who put me in that dress?"

HOW CAN YOU SAY THAT? I WAS DEAD, REMEMBER?

"Then who was responsible for my clothes?" asked Micah.

LET'S JUST SAY IT'S A GIFT TO KEEP YOU HUMBLE.

"Well, I am humbled!" said Micah. "But don't do that again."

FINE. NOW TEXT YOUR JOURNALS HOME.

Micah stuck his tongue out at the phone. He knew it was a silly thing to do, but he felt better afterward.

Micah typed:

HEAVENLY FATHER BLESSED US TO GET AWAY FROM THE POLICE IN PARIS. BATTERY ON THE PHONE WENT DEAD. PRAYED. GOD BLESSED US TO GET IT STARTED AGAIN. MY FAITH IS STRONGER.

He pushed SEND.
Alicia wrote:

JOHN GOT IN TROUBLE FOR PREACHING, BUT NONE OF US WENT TO JAIL. PHONE QUIT WORKING. I WAS SCARED AND FELT SORRY FOR MYSELF. WE PRAYED AND HEAVENLY FATHER SENT AN OLD WOMAN TO BE OUR FRIEND. WE RECHARGED THE SOLAR BATTERY WITH THE SUN.

She hit SEND.
Micah pressed the PRESENT button.

JOHN HAS COURAGE, D&C 82:10.

"You look this one up," said Alicia.
Micah pulled the scriptures up and scrolled to Doctrine and Covenants 82:10 and read, "The Lord is bound when we obey."

"John obeyed by preaching to the people, even though he would get in trouble from the police," said Alicia, "and he was blessed."

"Heavenly Father blessed us when we prayed," said Micah. "He helped us get the phone working again."

"The phone was dead, so we didn't get a picture this time," said Alicia. "I wish I had a photo of you in the dress and cape."

"I wouldn't be caught dead in the dress again," said Micah.

"Let's use the drawing program," said Alicia. "I want to draw a picture of John preaching to the people on the beach."

"I'll make one of him escaping the police," said Micah.

Each of them took a turn sketching on the phone. When they finished and entered them, the puzzle came onto the screen.

PUZZLE INCOMPLETE, said the phone. CENTER PIECE MISSING. The preaching and escape pictures were clustered in the "Courage" section with John ripping his shirt open for the men to tar and feather him.

"Oh no," said Alicia. "Will we ever get it?"

"I don't know what to do next," said Micah. "I have no idea what goes in the middle circle of the puzzle. And I don't know how to find out."

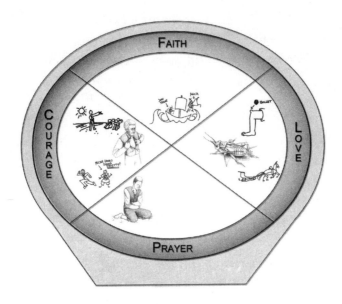

Micah swiped FUTURE EVENTS.

JOHN WRITES A BOOK, *THE GOVERNMENT OF GOD*.

"He sure writes a lot," said Alicia. "He's not only kind, but he's smart too."

MISSION TO NEW YORK.

PUBLISHED MORMON NEWSPAPER, *THE MORMON*.

"There's another newspaper," said Micah.

JUDGE AND LEGISLATOR IN UTAH

BRIGHAM YOUNG DIES AUGUST 29, 1877.

JOHN TAYLOR LEADS THE CHURCH AS PRESIDENT OF THE QUORUM OF THE TWELVE APOSTLES.

JOHN IS A KIND FATHER.

"John is kind," said Micah. "Maybe the center of the puzzle is his kindness. Let's try it."

"Good idea," said Alicia. "And we haven't even met any of his children."

They faded into the blackness.

10

FAMILY MAN

ALICIA landed on a dirt path just outside a white picket fence. Small houses made of mud bricks and logs lined the street. A horse and rider clip-clopped along the other side of the road. Children ran by, each rolling a large hoop with a stick. They looked like Hula-Hoops to Alicia.

She wore the same long pioneer dress with little blue checks that she had on when the Indians showed them how to find bulbs and make the gross burned cricket paste. She felt her neck and then her wrists. Still no necklace and CTR ring. She missed them.

"I love these overalls," said Micah. "I hated that tight French suit. These are loose and comfortable."

Micah checked his pockets and pulled out the phone. It lit up: SALT LAKE CITY, 1878.

A young man came around the corner. "Hello. I'm Matthias Cowley." He reached to shake their hands.

"Hi," said Micah. "I'm Micah, and this is my sister Alicia."

Matthias's mustache and beard matched his brown

hair, which was parted perfectly on the side. He looked dressed up in his dark homemade suit.

"Are you from around here?" asked Matthias.

"Just visiting," said Alicia.

"Until your family is assigned a settlement to homestead?"

How could Alicia answer that without telling a fib? She had to think quickly. "Uh, we're looking for . . . uh, President John Taylor."

"You're in luck," said Matthias. "His house is right here. I'm going teaching to his home right now.[1] Do you want to come with me?"

"Is that like home teaching?" asked Micah.

"We don't call it that," said Matthias. "We just call it teaching, but it's teaching in the home, so I guess you could call it home teaching."

I didn't know they had home teachers clear back at this time, thought Alicia.

They walked up to the door and knocked. An older boy opened the door.

"John W.," said Matthais, "this is Micah and Alicia."

"Welcome," said John W., pulling the door wide so they could come into the living room.

This must be one of John's sons, thought Alicia. His long-sleeved blue shirt and blue overalls looked comfortable, just like Micah said.

John sat at the table playing checkers with another son. He turned, "Micah and Alicia." Standing, he reached to give them both a hug. "It's nice to see you again. Come meet my family."

"Hello, President," said Matthias. He and John shook hands.

I'm glad I called him President when I talked to Matthias, thought Alicia. *I can only call him John in my head now.*

John pointed to his boys. "This is Brigham John Taylor and Ebenezer Young Taylor," said John, "but we call them Brig and Ebb. And you've already met John W."

"Hello," said Micah.

"Hi," said Alicia.

"I've come teaching," said Matthias.

"Fine! Sit down, please," said John.

Everyone clustered on the sofa and chairs around the room. Alicia sat next to Matthias. She looked at the round oak table in the middle of the room. *I'll bet John made this furniture himself,* thought Alicia. A braided rug covered the wooden floor, and lacy curtains decorated the small windows.

"I'd like to give a lesson on honesty and hard work," said Matthias.

"They go hand in hand," said John.

"Can you think of a few times you learned lessons in honesty?" Matthias asked the boys.

"Remember the time Angus Cannon's chickens got into the east lot," said Brig, "and Angus told us if we could catch them we could have them for the family to eat?"

"I remember," said Ebb. "We caught the chickens and sold them."

"We thought we were rich until Father found out," said Brig. "Then Father read to us from the Bible about paying back fourfold."[2]

"We had to earn enough to buy four times the chickens and give it to Angus Cannon," said Ebb.

"I even had to use the money I'd been saving for a new shirt," said Brig.

John laughed. "You learned your lesson, though. You've been very honest ever since."[3]

"We'll never do anything like that again," said Ebb.

Wow! thought Alicia. *Things are different now. If I take something and don't use it right, I just have to say sorry and give it back. I don't have to return four of them.* She looked at Micah. He must have been thinking the same thing because he raised his eyebrows and shook his head as if to say, "I can't believe it."

"Remember when Ezra decided to skip the Sunday afternoon meeting in the tabernacle?" asked John. "His friend was supposed to tell him who spoke so Ezra could report at family council, but his friend couldn't remember who talked."

"So Ezra said it was some old windbag." Ebb laughed.

"I got the biggest chuckle out of it," said John "I told him that old windbag was me."[4]

"He was so embarrassed," said Ebb, "that Father never had to say another word to him. Father knew he had skipped the sermon, and Ezra always attended the meetings after that."

Mom and Dad do the same thing with us, thought Alicia. *I always have to tell them what our Primary lesson was about, and we discuss the sacrament meeting talks every Sunday. I like doing it because it helps me remember the things I've heard. When we review them, I think of ways to be better during the week.*

"President Taylor," said Matthias, "you've taught us all to work hard too."

"Remember the garden?" said Brig, laughing.

"Father left town, and he assigned us to do the planting while he was gone," said John W.

"We all helped you with it so we could hurry and go play," said Matthias.

"But we were in such a rush that we just scattered the seeds wherever they landed," said Brig.

John turned to Micah and Alicia. "So when I came home and found the plants coming up in all sorts of odd places, I made them take it all out and plant again."

"He taught us to be proud of our work," said Brig.[5]

"Mom and Dad teach us the same way," said Alicia.

"Those are funny names for your parents," said Matthias.

"Oh, sorry," said Alicia, clapping her hand to her mouth. Would she ever learn to think before she talked? "When we plant a garden, *Mother* and *Father* always have us tie each end of a long string onto two sticks and shove them in the ground at either end of the row. Then we dig the furrow and plant the seeds evenly along the string in a straight line."

Matthias smiled. "We've learned a lot from you, President Taylor."

"I also assimilated some lessons from my children," said John.

Big words again, thought Alicia. But she kept quiet.

John continued. "Once Frederick W. got a novel from school, *20,000 Leagues Under the Sea*, by Jules Verne. I told him he shouldn't read novels. They were not good. So he put the book down and went to bed."

"Father was in for a surprise," said John W.

"I picked up the book just to look at it," said John,

"and read the first chapter. It was so good, I stayed up all night reading it."

"When Frederick got up in the morning," said John W., "he found Father just finishing it."

"True," said John. "I couldn't put the book down. So I told Frederick it was a fine book, and he could read it."[6]

A little girl ran in and climbed up on John's lap. "I want to feel the bullet in your knee, Papa, and will you tell me the story about Joseph Smith?" she asked.

John cuddled her into his arms and looked up at Alicia and Micah. "This is little Mary."

"And sing me a song, Papa."

Mary felt the bump. Alicia remembered Micah touched it very gently after the shooting because it was still healing. Everyone listened while John retold the story of the death of the Prophet Joseph Smith.

What a blessing it is to be here and see John alive, Alicia thought.

Mary snuggled closer into John's chest as he began to sing. His mellow voice filled the room. *"A poor wayfaring man of grief . . ."*

"Joseph loved this song, and it was Hyrum's favorite," whispered Matthias to Alicia.

Alicia wanted to tell Matthias that they were there when John was recovering from his wounds at Carthage, but she was silent. The music melted into Alicia's heart as John sang about giving a stranger food, drink, and clothes to keep him warm.

". . . The stranger started from disguise . . ."

"This is my favorite part," whispered Matthias. "The stranger was the Savior."

"... *These deeds shall thy memorial be; Fear not, thou didst them unto me.*"[7]

Wow, thought Alicia. *I guess Jesus really does watch everything I do. I would probably do more good deeds if I thought I was doing them for the Savior.*

"Thanks, Papa," said Mary. She jumped down from John's lap and ran outside. Alicia heard a dog bark.

John leaned forward in his chair, resting his elbows on his legs. "Now that you've taught me, Matthias, I want to teach all of you."

John looked at Micah and then Alicia. "Almost ten years ago we were meeting in the Tabernacle, and a man walked in the back door. He was a stranger in our midst, but I felt I knew him from somewhere. I studied his face for a few minutes and then I recognized him. It was Martin Harris—Book of Mormon witness!"

"He left the church for a long time, didn't he?" asked Matthias.

"Yes," said John. "He didn't come west with the Saints. But thirty-three years later, Elder Edward Stevenson brought him back to Salt Lake City and to the Church."[8]

"I'll bet you were glad to see him," said Micah.

"Well, I rushed down off the stand and threw my arms around him. We were so glad to see each other, we wept. At age eighty-three, he had to steady himself with a cane. We made our way to the stand, and I asked him to speak. He still bore a strong testimony of the Book of Mormon."[9]

John wiped a tear. "He was rebaptized, and I confirmed him a member of the Church."

Everyone in the room was quiet. John looked around

the circle. Alicia's eyes focused on him. "Martin Harris was honest with God. He knew he had seen an angel, and he could not deny it. He was true to the glorious vision he had."

"I'm glad he didn't deny his testimony of the angel showing him the golden plates." said Micah.

John smiled. "I was so happy he came back."

Alicia felt joy begin in her toes and spread through her entire body.

John leaned forward again. "It is proper that men should be honest with themselves, that they should be honest with each other."[10]

Alicia's eyes watered. She didn't need to see an angel to know the Book of Mormon was true. The Holy Ghost told her, and she would try to be true to that testimony and the Church all her life.

"Well," said John, taking a deep breath, "I have to go. I've got a meeting. Thank you for coming, Matthias." They shook hands.

Alicia put her arms around John's neck. "Thanks."

He kissed her cheek. "You are such an affable young lady."

"Big words again," said Alicia.

"Funny accent," said John.

Alicia giggled.

Micah shook John's hand. "Thank you. Maybe we'll see you again."

John smiled. "One of these days you are going to get home."

"I hope," said Micah.

Alicia skipped out the door, and Micah followed.

They walked down the street and around the corner.

"We didn't take a picture," said Micah, "but I couldn't without them seeing the phone."

"I know," said Alicia. "What does the phone tell us?

When Micah pressed the PRESENT button the puzzle appeared.

JOHN TAYLOR TEACHES HIS CHILDREN TO BE HONEST

NO PICTURE REQUIRED, the phone said. The outside ring around the scripture picture flashed red with the words "Honesty" and "Hard Work" in it.

"I try to be honest and work hard," said Alicia.

"Wow!" said Micah. "Honesty and hard work keep the picture together."

"It's cool," said Alicia. "But we still don't have the center."

"I know," said Micah. "I'm trying to have faith, but sometimes I just worry about how we'll get home."

FUTURE EVENTS lit the screen. Micah swiped it.

SUPERINTENDENT OF UTAH SCHOOLS, 1877–1881.

ORGANIZES PRIMARY AUGUST 1878.

PUBLISHES THE MEDIATION AND ATONEMENT.

"I didn't know John organized the Primary," said Alicia. "Let's try that. Maybe it's the center of the circle."

"We're almost to the end of John's life," said Micah. "Something has to be the middle of the puzzle. Did we miss it?"

"Maybe the Primary goes in the center," said Alicia.

Micah selected PRIMARY, and they faded into blackness.

11

STEALING MELONS

MICAH collapsed in a heap on a braided rag rug. A large desk loomed up in front of him. *This must be an office of some kind*, he thought. He looked down at his shirt and pants. They were the same clothes he'd had on when they visited John's house.

Alicia thudded onto the floor near him. "Where are we?"

"In some office," said Micah.

The phone lit up: AUGUST 1878.

"I guess that's when the Primary was organized," said Alicia. "If it's going to be organized today in a Church meeting, we're not very dressed up."

The phone buzzed in Micah's hand.

"What is it?" asked Alicia.

Micah looked. "A text from Dad."

"What does he say?"

"Where are you? I'm worried."

Micah's heart thumped into his stomach. "Dad's upset. Maybe we'll never get back." *Faith, I need to have faith*, he thought.

"Text back," said Alicia.

Micah typed:

WE HAVE TO SOLVE THIS PUZZLE YOU PUT ON THE PHONE BEFORE WE CAN GET HOME. WILL COME HOME AS SOON AS WE CAN.

He pushed SEND.

The phone lit up: TEXT WILL BE DOWNLOADED WHEN YOU RETURN HOME.

"No," said Micah. "We can't get a message to him? Why not?"

The phone was silent.

Micah clenched his fists but knew there was nothing he could do.

The office door opened, and John came in. He smiled. "Well, hello. I'm surprised to see you. Good morning to both of you."

"Hi," said Alicia.

"I'm glad you're still around," said John. "I could use your help today."

John walked to the other side of the room and pulled two chairs close to his desk.

"We can't get home, and we don't seem to be able to send a message to Dad, so we might as well help," muttered Micah to Alicia.

"That makes it sound like we'll only help if we can't do anything else," whispered Alicia.

"I didn't mean that," said Micah. He sighed and turned to John. "We'd love to help."

"Well, I have a problem," said John, motioning to the chairs he brought for Micah and Alicia. "We need to talk."

Lines of concern crowded John's forehead, and he rubbed his hands together. "I've just had a meeting with Sister Snow. She brought news from Bishop Hess and Sister Rogers about the children in Farmington."[1]

"What kind of news?" asked Alicia.

"Sister Rogers is worried about the boys," said John. "They're stealing melons from William Rice's farm and others in the area."

"That's not being honest," said Alicia.

"I know," said John. "Bishop Hess and Sister Rogers want permission to organize a Primary for the children. Bishop Hess has asked Sister Rogers and some of the other women in the Farmington Ward to teach the children about honesty and being polite to others."

"So what do you want us to do?" asked Micah.

"Could you make friends with a few of the boys, Micah, and help them see it's wrong to steal?"

"Sure," said Micah. "I'll try."

John turned to Alicia. "And would you get to know the girls? I understand they're hitching rides on the back of wagons as they roll through town. That's very dangerous."

"I'll help," said Alicia.

"You'll probably both meet Sister Rogers," said John. "She's contacting all the children to come to the first Primary meeting in a few days on August 25."[2]

"We'll go right now," said Micah.

"Come back and let me know what happens," said John. "And thank you for helping. I'm headed to another meeting. See you soon."

Micah pulled the phone from his pocket and typed FARMINGTON. "I guess the phone knows to send me to the melon patch and you to the wagons."

"We'll see," said Alicia. "Just don't leave me there. When you are ready to go, take me with you."

Micah grinned. "Have faith."

Alicia slugged him in the arm.

They faded into blackness.

Micah landed at the edge of a large patch of what looked like small watermelons.

"Get out of my field!" yelled a voice.

Micah stood up. "Who me?"

"Yes, you," said the man. He walked toward Micah. "Who are you, anyway? I don't recognize you."

"I-I'm just visiting for the day," stammered Micah.

"Don't steal any of my melons. Leave them alone," said the man.

"I won't take any," said Micah.

"Oh," said the man. "Well, boy's your age have been thieving from me, and I haven't got time to stand guard over my land. It takes a lot of hard work to grow and harvest melons." The man wiped his brow with the back of his sleeve. "I have all I can do right now to count and pick the tithing melons and take them to Brother Stayner at the Tithing office."[3] The man sighed. "Then I have the rest of the field to pick."

"Oh," said Micah. "Tithing? How do you know which ones are tithing melons?"

"I pick the biggest ones for tithing—every tenth melon."

Micah smiled at the man. "My name is Micah, and I'm *not* stealing."

"I'm sorry," said the man. "I'm so upset that I didn't introduce myself. My name is William Rice. It's nice to meet you."

"Same here," said Micah. "I'll see if I can find the boys and tell them to stop taking melons. Maybe we can even come back and help."

Micah turned, heading for the lane. He could see two boys leaning against a large tree in the distance. Micah walked up to them. "Hey," he said.

"Hay?" said one of the boys. "There's no hay here."

Micah bit his lip. That's the way he said hello to his friends at home. He'd forgotten where he was.

"Uh . . ." Micah hesitated.

"What's the matter? Cat got your tongue?" asked the other boy.

"I meant, 'Hello. I'm Micah.'"

"This is Victor, and I'm Jeremiah." One boy pointed to Victor and then himself.

"Nice to meet you."

"Where do you come from?" asked Victor. "You must be a stranger."

"I'm just visiting for the day."

"Want to help us? We're going to *borrow* a few of Brother Rice's melons," said Jeremiah.

"But that's stealing," said Micah.

"Look," said Victor, "we know the ropes around here, not you. As soon as Brother Rice goes in for lunch, we'll raid the field."[4]

"Taking things that are not yours is dishonest," said Micah.

"Oh, it's fine," said Jeremiah. "We do it all the time. I think he plants extra for us."

"Stealing isn't right," said Micah.

Jeremiah twisted his toe in the dirt. Micah could tell he was thinking about it.

"You're pullin' my leg, right?" said Victor.

"No," said Micah. "Brother Rice has a lot of work ahead of him, gathering the melons. If we help him, maybe he'll give us some melons for our work."

"Wait a minute," said Victor. "I smell a rat."

"Oh, stop with the silly talk, Victor," said Jeremiah, clenching his fists. "You're doing it just to impress Micah. You don't usually speak that way."

Victor turned to Jeremiah and laughed. "Got you upset, didn't I?"

Jeremiah rolled his eyes and shook his head.

Here was Micah's chance. Could he talk the boys into helping? *Heavenly Father, please bless me to know what to say*, he thought. "Let's offer to help Brother Rice count the tithing melons and take them to Brother Stayner."

"Now why would I want to get myself into a lot of work?" asked Victor. "I'm supposed to be home putting up the hay right now, anyway."

"Maybe we should offer help," said Jeremiah. "Just for fun. I'd love to see the look on Brother Rice's face. He thinks we're trouble."

"Well," said Victor, "we are trouble. And I don't want to pick the whole patch."

"Let's just gather his tithing for him," said Micah. "That's at least some help."

"Watch his face when we tell him," said Jeremiah.

The boys walked towards Brother Rice in the field.

Brother Rice stood. "You boys are pure mischief. What do you want?"

"We'd like to pick your tithing melons," said Micah.

"What?" asked Brother Rice, raising his eyebrows and tightening his neck muscles. "I don't believe you."

Victor smiled.

"Micah talked us into helping you," said Victor. "It's better than putting up the hay."

Brother Rice scratched his head and raised his eyebrows again. "Well, knock my socks off, boys! Go ahead and help."

Victor burst out laughing.

"What's so funny?" asked Brother Rice.

"Nothing," said Jeremiah, pulling Victor toward the wheelbarrow.

"We got a rise out of him," said Victor. "He made a face *and* used a silly saying."

You need to learn some manners, thought Micah.

"Be sure you take every tenth melon," said Brother Rice, "and only the biggest ones."

"We know," said Jeremiah.

The boys filled wheelbarrow after wheelbarrow and rolled them to the back of the wagon to unload. Brother Rice hitched the horse when they were done.

"Thanks, boys," he said. "Each of you take a melon for your lunch. You've earned it."

They walked back into the patch and picked out a juicy melon.

"I used to hate work," said Micah. "I'd get out of it every chance I could."

"There you have it folks, straight from the horse's mouth," said Victor, bowing and laughing.

Victor is a nut, thought Micah. *And sometimes he doesn't make sense.*

"I wouldn't say I like work," said Jeremiah.

"I know how you feel," said Micah, remembering times when he'd skipped out of doing his chores. "But it's fun now." Something had changed inside him. He didn't know exactly what it was. Maybe he'd grown up a little.

As the boys walked down the road, Victor broke his melon open and took a big juicy bite. "I think this tastes better since it isn't stolen."

Exactly, thought Micah.

Along the path, a woman hurried toward them.

"It's Sister Rogers," whispered Victor. "She's going to invite us to a new meeting called 'Primary' to keep us out of trouble."

Primary keeps me out of trouble, thought Micah, *and it's cool.*

"Hello, boys," said Sister Rogers. "I'd like to invite you to a gathering for the young people on the

JOHN TAYLOR AND THE MYSTERY PUZZLE

twenty-fifth of August. We're going to have Bible study, songs, skits, recitations and other enjoyable things. Will you come?"

"Ma will make me," mumbled Victor.

"We'll come," said Jeremiah.

"Fine," said Sister Rogers. "See you there." She hurried on down the street.

12

WAGON RIDES

ALICIA landed in the middle of a shady lane. *This must be Farmington*, she thought. She watched some girls across the street playing jump rope with two ropes, turning in opposite directions at the same time. *That looks hard*, she thought.

A horse pulling a wagon clip-clopped down the road.

"It's your turn to chase the wagon and ride, Olive," said the oldest girl.[1]

Alicia watched the littlest girl with dark curly hair leave the jump rope and run into the road behind a wagon piled high with hay. She raced after it and grabbed the back floorboards, running fast to keep up. She tried to jump up onto the cart, but she wasn't tall enough. Holding on, she let her feet drag on the ground. The wagon carried her along until lost her grip and fell. She smacked face first in the dirt. A sob escaped her chest. She stood and spit dirt, then brushed the dust from her eyes and nose. Snuffling, she walked back to the others.

"Better luck next time," called the oldest girl. "Harriet, you're next."

"I know it's my turn," said a girl in a green checked dress.

Olive looked at the oldest girl. "Don't be so bossy, Lucy."

"I'm not bossy," said Lucy. "I'm just keeping you in line."

"We don't need a line," said Harriet. "There are only three of us."

Another horse and wagon came down the street. Harriet waited, her eyes focused on the back of the wagon. As it passed her, she ran and jumped up onto the end. The driver turned his head and frowned at her. Harriet rode past two houses and jumped off.

"My turn," said Lucy. Alicia watched her jump on the back of the next wagon just like Harriet had done. The driver didn't notice her.

"My turn again," said Olive.

Another wagon came along, pulled by two horses. It was piled high with corn and going faster than the others had.

"You can't catch that one," said Lucy. "It's going too fast."

"No it's not," said Olive, racing into the street. She ran after the wagon clear to the corner, but she couldn't catch it. As she turned to walk back, a horse and rider galloped from the side street onto the main road headed right for Olive. She froze.

Oh no! thought Alicia.

The rider saw Olive and reined his horse in hard. The animal whinnied and reared. Olive fell back and screamed. The horse's hooves pawed the air and came down hard, narrowly missing her. She scrambled to the side of the road, crying. The driver galloped away, shaking his head.

Alicia ran down the block and across the street to Olive. "Are you all right?"

"I skinned my elbow," she whimpered.

"Chasing wagons is dangerous." Alicia put her arm around Olive and helped dust her off. They walked toward the others. Alicia wiped a tear from Olive's cheek.

The girls hurried toward them.

"Are you hurt?" asked Lucy.

"No," said Olive. "Well, my elbow is skinned." A trickle of blood ran down her arm.

"Thank goodness that horse didn't step on you," said Harriet.

"I was so worried," said Alicia.

Olive looked up at Alicia with a questioning look. "I don't know you."

"My name's Alicia."

"I'm Olive, and these are my friends."

"Welcome to Farmington," said Lucy. "Did you just move here?"

"I'm visiting," said Alicia. "Running after those wagons seems very scary."

"You can get hurt," said Olive, rubbing her elbow. "But what else can we do?"

"I hear Sister Wilcox is melting wax from her beehives, and she's going to make candles," said Harriet. "Maybe we can help."

"I'd like to learn how to do that," said Alicia.

"I like working," said Lucy. "Sometimes we chase wagons just because we're bored and it's exciting."

"Oh, there's Sister Rogers," said Harriet, looking down the street.

Alicia could see a lady coming towards them, stopping at each house along the way to talk to the children and their mothers. She hurried toward the girls.

"Hello, girls," said Sister Rogers. "I'd like to invite you to our first Primary meeting on the twenty-fifth, which is tomorrow. Can you come?"

"What kind of meeting is it?" asked Lucy.

"We'll learn lots of new things," said Sister Rogers. "We'll have recitations and songs. We'll learn about manners and write plays and skits."

"That sounds fun," said Olive. "I want to come."

"We'll come too," said Harriet, looking at Lucy.

"Good," said Sister Rogers. "See you soon."

"Primary is my favorite," said Alicia.

They turned down the next street. "How do you know?" asked Harriet.

Uh-oh, thought Alicia. *I have to keep my mouth shut.* She wanted to tell her new friends all about Activity Days and the fun things they did, but she couldn't. "Oh, I-I . . . the things Sister Rogers told us about are my favorite things to do."

"Mine, too," said Olive, catching Alicia's hand. "Sister Wilcox's house is just over there." She pointed. "Come on."

Lucy knocked at the door. A tall, slender woman with brown hair pulled back in a tight bun answered the door. Her apron looked starched and white.

"Hello," said Sister Wilcox. "What can I do for you?"

"My mother told me you were melting your beeswax today to dip candles," said Harriet. She glanced at the others. "We'd like to help you, but you'll have to show us what to do."

"Oh, that would be wonderful," said Sister Wilcox. "I feel like I need four hands to get everything done."

In the backyard were four metal buckets.

Sister Wilcox pointed to the first bucket. A wooden frame holding a honeycomb rested over the top of the bucket like a lid. "Honey is draining out of the wax in this wooden frame. As soon as all the honey has dripped out of the honeycomb, then I cut the wax out of the wooden frame and put it in this second bucket where, as you can see, it's melting over a slow fire."

Alicia fanned herself with her hand. It was a hot August day, and the fire made it even hotter. She looked in the bucket. The wax was almost dissolved into a yellow liquid.

A pool of wax dripped through a cloth into the next bucket.

"I've clipped a feed sack to the edges of this bucket to strain the wax so it will be clean enough to make candles."

Sister Wilcox pointed to the last bucket. "This wax is ready for dipping the candles."

She led them to a small tree branch that held six strings as long as two candle lengths draped over it. "These are the candle wicks. If you pick up the middle of the wick hanging on the branch, you can dip it into the wax so each side of the wick will make a candle— two candles at once. Then hang it back on the branch to cool. Dip it quickly so the hot wax doesn't melt the wax that's already on the candle. By the time you've dipped all six strings, the first one will be cool enough to dip again."

"I'm afraid to dip the candles," said Olive. "The wax is hot, and I don't want to get burned."

"You just hold the candles by the wick at the top and dip it in," said Sister Wilcox. "Your hand will stay above the hot wax."

"I'll help you when it's your turn," said Harriet.

"Each of you take care of one of the buckets, and then change off when you need a rest."

Alicia started with the candle dipping. She made up a little chant in her head. "Dip, hang, cool. Dip, hang, cool." Every time she dipped the candles a little more wax stuck to the wick and the candles grew fatter. It was fun.

Alicia concentrated. Dip, hang, cool. Dip, hang, cool.

A loud "Psssst," came from the bushes.

Alicia jumped and turned around. Micah snapped her picture.

"Don't scare me! And don't take my picture before I'm ready!"

"Let's go," he said.

"I have to tell Sister Wilcox," said Alicia. She finished the rotation, left the candles to cool, and found Sister Wilcox hanging clothes on the line. "My brother has come for me. I need to go."

Sister Wilcox finished draping a bed sheet over the line and turned to her. "Thank you so much for helping."

"You're welcome," said Alicia. She turned to the girls, "My brother is here. I have to go."

"I'll dip the candles," said Lucy.

"I'll miss you," said Olive. "Thanks for helping me."

"I'll see you in Primary tomorrow," said Alicia.

"Tomorrow," said Lucy.

"We'll be there," said Harriet.

Micah and Alicia walked down the street.

The phone lit up: FIRST PRIMARY MEETING.

Micah swiped and they faded into blackness.

They landed in the bushes outside a rock church. *Our church is made of bricks*, thought Alicia. Children darted in and around the trees and shrubs. Micah and Alicia made their way through the crowd of kids into the building, where Alicia overheard two leaders talking.

"I think there are over a hundred boys and a hundred girls here," one woman said. [2]

"Wonderful," said the other leader.

Alicia and Micah entered the chapel. Sister Rogers stood in the front, arranging everyone by age. The littlest children slid into the front benches, and the older boys and girls at the back. Alicia looked for Harriet and Lucy and Olive. Since they were different ages, they sat in separate classes. She waved at them and slipped into the row by Lucy.

Micah joined Victor and Jeremiah with the boys on the back row.

After everyone found a place to sit, Sister Rogers walked to the podium. "Welcome, children. It is wonderful to have you here. You are our jewels, and we want the angels to guard and protect you.³ What would this world be without the love you bring to it?"⁴

The little children wiggled in their seats. One small girl took her shoe off and twirled it on her toe.

Alicia covered her mouth with her hand and giggled to herself.

"Let's learn the first Article of Our Faith together," said Sister Rogers. "Those of you who know it, say it with me."

Alicia repeated it along with Sister Rogers and some of the other leaders. "We believe in God the Eternal Father and in His Son Jesus Christ and in the Holy Ghost."

Lucy turned to Alicia. "How do you know that?"

Alicia felt surprised that Lucy didn't say it. None of the girls in her row seemed to know it. At home, all the Primary kids her age, and a lot younger, knew at least the first Article of Faith. "We have to memorize all the Articles of Faith in Primary," said Alicia.

Lucy looked puzzled.

Alicia clapped her hand over her mouth. "Uh, I mean I learned them so I could recite them when I come to Primary." That was the truth. Alicia did learn the Articles of Faith to say in Primary.

Lucy frowned.

I forgot to keep my mouth shut again, thought Alicia.

Everyone repeated the Article of Faith until the older children knew it.

"I can say it," whispered Lucy, smiling.

Alicia grinned back.

Sister Rogers walked to the podium. "Let's sing, 'In Our Lovely Deseret.'"[5]

Everyone sang. *This is almost like Primary at home,* thought Alicia. *But there are no pictures or games for singing time. Primary is just beginning, so I guess they don't have those yet.*

"Next we'll have a skit on manners," said Sister Rogers.[6] "Older boys, please come to the front."

After the skit, everyone sang another song; and the meeting was dismissed.

Micah tapped Alicia on the shoulder and whispered in her ear. "The phone just buzzed, and we need to go back to John's office. Let's slip out the side door."

"See you," said Alicia to Lucy. "I've got to go."

Micah and Alicia hurried outside, and Micah swiped JOHN TAYLOR'S OFFICE.

Through the blackness, they landed next to John's desk.

"Hello," John said. "How did it go?"

"Fine," said Micah. He told John about Brother Rice and the boys.

Alicia explained the dangers of riding the wagons, and then how the girls helped dip candles.

They both described the first Primary meeting.

"Thank you for showing the youth about service," said John. "I'm grateful. I know Primary will teach the children of the Church about faith."

"Sister Rogers helped them memorize the first Article of Faith," said Alicia.

"I guess you're referring to the Articles of Our Faith that are printed in the Pearl of Great Price. There's a new edition out this year."[7]

"In our time, we call them Articles of Faith," said Micah.

"And we memorize them all in Primary," said Alicia.

"I'm so thankful that Primary will bless children's lives in coming years," said John.

"I love Primary," said Alicia.

"I've learned a lot," said Micah. "I'm trying to have faith, and I'm also working on being kind and generous like you."

"Maybe you'll get home now," said John.

Alicia hugged John, and Micah shook his hand.

"See you," said Alicia.

They waved as they walked into the sunshine and found a quiet shady street where they could sit on the lawn and see if their Primary pictures fit the middle of the puzzle.

The phone lit up: TEXT YOUR JOURNALS HOME.

Micah typed:

TAUGHT THE BOYS ABOUT HONESTY AND TITHING. IT FEELS GOOD TO HELP A PROPHET. I'M GLAD I COULD GO TO THE FIRST PRIMARY MEETING. JOHN SAYS PRIMARY TEACHES US ABOUT FAITH.

Micah hit SEND.

Alicia typed:

I DON'T WANT TO RUN AFTER WAGONS IN THE STREET. IT'S TOO SCARY. I HAD FUN DIPPING CANDLES. I

WENT TO THE FIRST PRIMARY MEETING. I LOVE PRIMARY.

Alicia hit SEND and pressed the PRESENT button.

SCRIPTURE PICTURE
COMPLETE FOUR SECTIONS, PLUS THE CENTER KEY

PRIMARY ORGANIZED UNDER JOHN'S DIRECTION. CHILDREN LEARN ABOUT FAITH. ETHER 12:6.

"I'll look this one up," said Alicia. She pulled the scriptures up and scrolled to the Book of Mormon and found Ether. She read, "Faith is things which are hoped for and not seen; wherefore, dispute not because ye see not, for ye receive no witness until after the trial of your faith."

"Did the pioneer children learn about faith in Primary?" asked Micah.

"I don't know," said Alicia.

"Maybe the boys will find out about being honest and working hard and paying tithing."

"I hope the girls decided to be helpful, like dipping candles." Alicia thought for a minute. "I think faith means being honest, paying tithing, and serving others."

"I wish my faith would just automatically stay strong," said Micah. "But I know it doesn't work that way."

The puzzle appeared on the screen. Pictures of the melons and candles slid into the faith section next to Alicia's drawing of John standing on the boat in the storm on his way to Canada.

PUZZLE INCOMPLETE, said the screen.

"No," said Micah. "This was supposed to be the

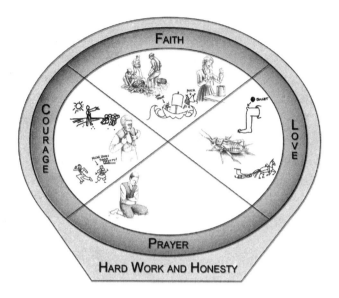

center of the circle. What'll we do now? We've got to get home. Dad is worried."

"Maybe the phone is teaching us about faith," said Alicia.

"I try to have faith," said Micah. "But what do we do next? I'm out of ideas."

"I don't know," said Alicia. "Let's ask the phone."

Micah raised his hands above his head. "Yes! It's a great idea. Why didn't we think of that before?"

Alicia typed, WHAT DO WE DO NOW?

The phone lit up: I THOUGHT YOU'D NEVER ASK!

INQUIRE ABOUT THE SCRIPTURE THAT GOES WITH THE CENTER PICTURE.

"The phone's using big words like John," said Alicia, giggling. She typed: GIVE US THE SCRIPTURE FOR THE CENTER PICTURE, PLEASE.

REVELATION 14:6.

"Where is Revelation?" asked Micah.

"I don't know," said Alicia. "Let me look it up." She scrolled through the Book of Mormon. "It's not here. And I know it's not in the Doctrine and Covenants."

"How about the Bible?"

"Good idea," said Alicia. She swiped through the Old Testament. "Not here."

"New Testament," said Micah.

Alicia scrolled through the books. "There it is. The last book in the New Testament."

Micah looked over her shoulder. "Chapter 14, verse 6." He read: "And I saw another angel fly in the midst of heaven, having the everlasting gospel to preach unto them that dwell on the earth, and to every nation, and kindred, and tongue, and people."

"I think it's talking about the angel Moroni," said Alicia.

"Where are we going to find the angel Moroni?" asked Micah.

"On the temples, silly," said Alicia.

"Did John dedicate a temple?" asked Micah.

"I don't know," said Alicia. She stroked the key pad to find FUTURE EVENTS. She swiped it.

DEDICATES LOGAN UTAH TEMPLE, MAY 1884.

"There it is," said Micah. "That's where we'll get our picture."

Alicia swiped, and they swirled into blackness.

13

WHERE'S THE ANGEL?

ALICIA tumbled onto the grass between a yellow brick house and a white picket fence. She wore a lovely white dress with soft blue flowers on it. She could feel a tie in the back and looked over her shoulder to see a big blue bow. Her sun bonnet matched her dress. *Wow! I'm an old fashioned sunbonnet girl,* thought Alicia, smiling. Micah landed nearby in a dark suit with a white shirt and black bow tie.

Alicia squinted into the bright sun. Across the street stood a tall stone building. Light glanced off the high arched windows, giving the structure a heavenly appearance. The Logan Temple seemed to watch over the whole valley.

Wagons and buggies stood along the road. An older girl and a younger boy struggled to unload a trunk from the back of a wagon. Micah walked toward the girl. "Can we help you?"

"Thanks," she said. "We came yesterday and just haven't unloaded this trunk yet. It has the white temple clothes for my twelve brothers and sisters. After the dedication, we're going to be sealed in the temple."

"Wow," said Alicia. "That's a lot of kids."

"What?" asked the girl. "Kids are baby goats, not children."

"Oops," said Alicia. "Sorry. It's just a code language between me and my brother."

"Yes," said Micah, raising his eyebrows and looking at Alicia. "It's code talk."

"Code talk?" asked the girl.

How are we going to get out of this one? wondered Alicia. *Change the subject,* she thought. "My name's Alicia. What's yours?"

The girl smiled, flipping her long red curls to the side of her freckled face. "I'm Arabella, and this is my brother Adam."

Micah extended his hand. "I'm Micah. Nice to meet you." He walked to the back of the wagon and helped Adam lift the trunk out.

"Where do you want it?" asked Micah.

"Over there on my uncle's veranda," said Adam, pointing to the yellow brick house. Children ran around on a big porch lined with wicker rocking chairs and cushioned benches.

Micah and Adam set the trunk next to a rocking chair near the front steps.

"Thanks," said Arabella.

"Where do you come from?" asked Alicia.

"We're from Oakley, Idaho," said Arabella. "We've traveled for five days to get here."

"I'll bet you're tired," said Micah.

"We are," said Adam. "But we're so happy to be sealed as a family."

"We can hardly wait," said Arabella. "It's such a

blessing to have a temple so close."

Alicia could see tears in Arabella's eyes. *Five days,* Alicia thought. *That's a long trip. They traveled five days, and they think the temple is close. I guess it is for them. The only other temple is St. George, and that's really far away. When we went to Disneyland last year, it only took us one day to get there.* She and Micah lived near a temple— only twenty minutes away. As soon as she was twelve, she would be able to do baptisms for the dead whenever she wanted.

I need to be more grateful that we have a temple close, she thought.

"We'll be thinking of you in the temple," said Alicia. "Your whole family there—how wonderful!"

"Thanks," said Arabella again. "Oh, I'm just making hot biscuits. Would you like some?"

Alicia noticed a delicious aroma coming from the house. "They sure smell good."

"They're my specialty," said Arabella.

Pioneer girls like Arabella didn't have time to jump on the back of wagons, thought Alicia. With thirteen kids, there was probably plenty to do. She wanted to be that kind of a girl—a hard worker.

"Thanks," said Micah. "Maybe just one, and then we need to meet someone."

Arabella ran into the house and came back with a plate of hot biscuits smothered with butter and honey.

Micah bit into one. "This is the best I've ever tasted."

Alicia slid one off the dish and nibbled the edges. Sweetness spilled around inside her mouth and over her tongue before she swallowed. *This is better than my chocolate birthday cake last month,* she thought.

"You're a good cook," said Micah. "If I lived in Oakley, I'd come to your house often."

Arabella blushed. "Thanks."

Alicia finished her biscuit and licked her fingers. "That was yummy. Thanks."

"Yummy?" Arabella looked puzzled.

"Uh, code talk again," said Micah. "We have to go. Thanks." They walked across the street.

"My mouth always gets me in trouble," said Alicia.

Micah smiled at her. "I've never thought about being far from a temple."

"I was thinking the same thing. Arabella was so happy, she had tears in her eyes. I don't feel that way when I talk about the temple. It's just always there. I need to be more thankful."

"And they said it was close—five days away. That's far, I think." Micah pulled the phone from his pocket. The screen lit: MAY 17, 1884, LOGAN TEMPLE DEDICATION.[1]

Alicia studied both the towers of the temple. "I don't see angel Moroni on the top."

"Oh, it must be there," said Micah. "Angel Moroni is on all the temples."

"Well, I don't see him," said Alicia, "but take a picture of the temple anyway."

"He's got to be there," said Micah, looking again and snapping a picture. "Maybe the phone won't care."

The phone buzzed. YES I WILL.

"No, no, no," said Micah, slapping his hand to his forehead. "This can't be happening to us. What are we going to do?"

"I guess find John," said Alicia. "Even if it isn't the right picture, I want to go to the dedication."

"Fine." Micah frowned. "But how are we *ever* going to get home?"

"Where's your faith?" asked Alicia. "Remember John standing on the deck of the boat in the storm? He had faith that Heavenly Father would bless him. We've been okay so far."

"I guess." Micah scuffed the grass with his shoe.

Alicia looked at the scowl on his face. "It's like you have a big black cloud over your head."

"I'm upset!" said Micah.

They walked the path to the front of the building. Flowers of all colors lined the carriage drive. People shuffled back and forth in a long line to get into the temple. John stood by the door.

"Let's ask John about the angel," said Alicia, rushing up to him. "John . . ."

The man standing next to John frowned at her.

Oops, she thought. "Or maybe I should call you President Taylor." Now was definitely not a good time to ask.

John laughed and hugged her. "I'm so glad to see you. You're like my little girl. You can always call me John." He turned to the man standing beside him. "This is President Card."

Alicia squeezed John's hand and turned to President Card. "Pleased to meet you." She curtsied to make sure he thought she was polite. She didn't like anyone frowning at her.

"Good morning, Micah," said John.

"Hello, President," said Micah, smiling.

Micah must have gotten himself together, thought Alicia. *He doesn't seem upset anymore.*

John winked at Micah and said to President Card, "Tell the ushers to open the doors wide for the Saints and be sure to check each ticket before they let anyone enter."

"Yes, President Taylor," said President Card.

John turned to Alicia and Micah. "The two of you, come with me." He led them through the temple doors to the east pulpit, where they stood watching hundreds of people file in. President Card joined them.

John studied the crowd. Suddenly he turned to President Card and whispered. "See that woman coming through the doorway? Don't let her in. She's not worthy."

"She must have a ticket," whispered President Card, "or she couldn't get in."

"I don't know what the problem is, but the Spirit of God tells me she's not worthy."

President Card left the stand

and greeted the woman in line. Alicia could see him talking to her, and soon he and the woman left the building.

When President Card returned, John asked, "What was the matter?"

"She is a nonmember who paid a dollar to an inactive member for the ticket," said President Card.[2] "She was curious to see what the dedication would be like."

"Wow," whispered Alicia to Micah. "John really has the Spirit with him to pick her out of this huge crowd of people."

"I know," said Micah. "I want to be good enough to have the Spirit with me like that. I guess I have to start with having more faith."

John stood at the pulpit and called the meeting to order. Micah and Alicia sat in the front row. Everyone quieted. The choir sang, and Alicia felt happy and peaceful inside.

She looked at John. A light seemed to shine from his face as he rose to offer the dedicatory prayer.[3] Her breath caught, and tears came to her eyes. *I'm so grateful to belong to this Church and be friends with this great prophet*, she thought.

John began to speak. "We dedicate [this house] that Thy servants may go forth to the nations of the earth endowed with power from on high . . . according to Thy word. . . . that thy servants . . . may become saviors upon Mount Zion."[4] Alicia wondered if John remembered the dream he had as a child of the angel flying through the heavens, sending a message to all the earth. And now he preached about that very thing.

". . . And, as all wisdom dwells with thee . . . we

humbly seek . . . Thy blessing to rest upon this house, that it may be indeed a house of learning under . . . direction and inspiration. . . We pray also that the . . . Holy Ghost . . . may be our guide and instructor."[5]

Micah reached over and squeezed her hand and smiled. Alicia could tell he was happy to be here too.

". . . and that Thine angels may be permitted to visit this holy habitation and communicate . . . the interests of the living and the dead."[6]

Oh, thought Alicia. *I can't wait until I'm twelve and can go to the temple. I wonder if an angel will come to be with me. Maybe I won't see an angel, but I'll feel its presence.*

"I'm so thankful for temples," whispered Micah.

Alicia smiled. "Me too."

When the meeting was over, Alicia found John and hugged him. "I don't want to leave the temple."

John smiled down at her. "I don't want to leave either. That's why I'm going to come to the temple as often as I can."

Everyone shook hands and talked in hushed tones.

As they walked outside, Micah said to John, "We need to find a temple with a statue of the angel Moroni on the top."

"Oh?" said John. "That's an interesting question. There hasn't been an angel Moroni on any of the temples so far. We plan to put one on the Salt Lake Temple, but that's a ways off."

"No angels at all?" asked Micah.

"Now, I didn't say that," said John. "Just no angel Moroni. There was a flying angel, holding a trumpet in one hand and a book in the other, placed on the Nauvoo

Temple tower, but I don't think it was ever said to be the angel Moroni."

"Oh," said Alicia.

"Why do you ask?" said John.

"Because we can't get back home until we find a picture that goes with Revelation 14:6."

John looked down at them and smiled. "'And I saw another angel fly in the midst of heaven, having the everlasting gospel to preach unto them that dwell on the earth, and to every nation, and kindred, and tongue, and people.' That scripture doesn't mention the angel Moroni specifically."

"Yes," said Micah, pumping his fist. "The pho . . . black box didn't say it had to be angel Moroni. We did." The phone buzzed in his pocket, and he pulled it out.

YOU CATCH ON QUICK, the screen said.

"Duh," said Alicia to herself.

"We have to go," said Micah.

Tears came to Alicia's eyes. "I don't think you'll see us again," she said to John. "It's for sure this time. With the help of prayer, we'll get home now."

"We'll see you when you were younger in Nauvoo," said Micah, "but you won't see us again in your lifetime."

"That's so hard for me to understand," said John. "But I trust you're right. I've loved being friends with you. I'll look down on your time when I'm in Heaven and think of you."

Alicia wiped her wet cheek. "I'll miss you."

John pulled her close and hugged her. "I'll miss you too—even with your funny accent."

Alicia giggled.

"Thanks." Micah shook John's hand.

Alicia looked back and waved as they walked away. But John didn't notice. He was surrounded by other people.

"I can't believe it." Micah hurried over to sit under a poplar tree on the grass.

"Just remember," said Alicia, clearing her throat with a sense of importance, "*I* was the one who wanted to go to the Nauvoo Temple dedication."

"You're right," said Micah. "I should listen better. Let's hurry so we can get back to Nauvoo."

The phone lit up: TEXT YOUR JOURNALS HOME.

Micah wrote: I NEED TO LISTEN AND HAVE MORE FAITH. I FELT THE SPIRIT IN THE TEMPLE DEDICATION I LOVE BEING IN THE TEMPLE.

Alicia wrote: I'M GOING TO THE TEMPLE AS SOON AS I'M TWELVE. ANGELS MAY BE THERE WITH ME. I LOVE THE TEMPLE. JOHN IS A PROPHET OF GOD. I'M THANKFUL FOR HIM.

Micah pressed the PRESENT button, and the wheel appeared.

SCRIPTURE PICTURE
COMPLETE FOUR SECTIONS, PLUS THE CENTER KEY

The phone lit up: THROUGH PRAYER, JOHN TAYLOR TRUSTS IN THE LORD, PROVERBS 3:5.

"Better let me look that one up," said Micah. "Whatever it says, I need it." He scrolled to the Old Testament and put his finger on Proverbs 3:5.

Alicia leaned over his shoulder.

"Trust in the Lord with all thine heart," he read. "I have to trust the Lord more than I do. I want to remember to do that, but sometimes I forget."

"We all forget," said Alicia. "Don't be so hard on yourself."

The picture of the Logan Temple slid into the "Prayer" section of the wheel to the side of praying in the woods in England.

"Now for the center," said Micah.

FUTURE EVENTS lit the screen.

"No," said Micah to the phone. "We need the past. Can we go backward?"

"Yes," said Alicia. "Remember when we left the ship in the storm and got to the tar and feathering? We went back to see what other things John had done."

"But we didn't try to see those things; we just read about them." Micah looked at his hands. "You know

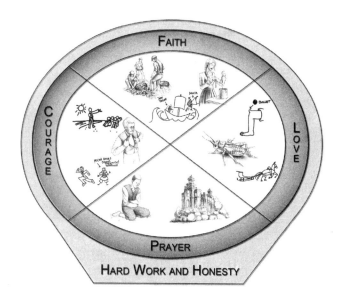

what? Let's pray about this. We still haven't got it figured out."

Leaving the shade of the poplar tree, they found a quiet wooded area down the hill and across the street from the temple. They knelt in prayer.

When they arose, Alicia had a strong feeling that the phone would help them. "The phone has always helped us when we've asked it. Let's see what it says."

Micah typed: HOW DO WE GET TO THE NAUVOO TEMPLE?

THANKS FOR ASKING! appeared on the screen.

"Smart aleck," said Micah.

The phone ignored him. WHEN PAST, PRESENT, AND FUTURE APPEAR ON THE SCREEN, PRESS PAST AND THEN TYPE IN 'ORIGINAL NAUVOO TEMPLE.'

"That makes sense," said Alicia. "We don't want to go to the present-day Nauvoo Temple because John won't be there."

"And we have to hurry," said Micah. "Dad is worried."

Micah typed, and they faded into blackness.

14

THE ANGEL

MICAH landed on the path in front of the Nauvoo Temple. The phone buzzed:

JULY 1845. TEMPLE WILL BE DEDICATED MAY 1, 1846.[1]
Alicia dropped beside Micah.

People strolled around the temple grounds, some dodging lumber being carried into the temple or wagonloads of rocks. Others laid out blankets for a picnic away from the saws, hammers, and chisels. Children ran everywhere.

"They're having a celebration of some kind," said Alicia.

"But the temple won't be dedicated for almost a year," said Micah.

"Look," said Alicia. "They're finishing that tower on the top, but there's no angel."

"I can hear workmen up there," said Micah.

"Let's see if we can find John."

"I wonder where the angel is," said Micah

They ran into the temple and found the stairs.

"We should walk," said Alicia. "It's the temple."

"You're right." Micah slowed to a fast jog up the stairs.

"That's almost a run," said Alicia. "I can hardly keep up with you."

Micah's breath came in sharp short bursts. *These are steep stairs*, he thought. As they climbed, the workmen's voices became louder. Was John's one of them?

"Delicious," said a voice.

"I grew this same variety of watermelon," said another, "but mine aren't this sweet."

Bang, bang, bang hammered above their heads.

"Sounds like people are eating and working," said Alicia.

At the top of the stairs, Micah peeked his head around the corner into the tower room. John sat, eating watermelon with a group of men. His hair was brown instead of gray, as it was when they saw him in Logan. *He* is *younger*, thought Micah.

John jumped from his chair. "Micah! Is Alicia with you?"

"Hi," said Micah. "Yes, she's here."

"Wonderful," said John. "Let me introduce you."

Micah and Alicia stepped into the tall room. Sawdust littered the floor with scraps of boards here and there. The men sat on wooden chairs scattered around the room, eating melon.

"These are my friends, Micah and Alicia," said John. "They cared for me during my recovery after Carthage."

Micah smiled. "Hello."

John continued. "This is Joseph Hovey, George Smith, Willard Richards, Heber Kimball, William Walker, and Stephen Goddard."[2]

Micah knew some of the men. He remembered meeting Heber Kimball and Willard Richards with Brigham Young. He hoped they didn't recognize him. What would he say if they did?

"Nice to meet you," said Alicia.

"You seem very familiar," said Brother Kimball. "Do you live in Nauvoo?"

"Oh, I-I . . . not in the city," said Micah. *Help!* he thought.

Alicia glanced at him. "We'd really like a piece of watermelon."

"We've got extra," said John. "I should have offered you some."

"Thanks," said Micah, relieved. "What's the celebration?"

John handed them each a piece. "The cupola is finished."[3]

Alicia pulled on John's sleeve, "Big words again. What's a kyoo-puh-luh?"

John smiled and pointed overhead. "It's the dome with a steeple on the top. The workmen just hammered the last nail in place. Isn't it beautiful?"

"Yes," said Alicia. "It's lovely."

Micah slurped a juicy bite of the melon.

"In fact, it's so amazing . . ." said Stephen Goddard. "Watch me." He ran his hands through his sandy brown hair and cinched his belt tighter around his thin waist.

"What?" asked Brother Richards.

Brother Goddard ascended the steep stairs inside the lower section of the cupola, and the others followed.

"Where are you going?" John asked Brother Goddard.

"Just watch," said Brother Goddard.

John turned to Alicia and Micah. "We'll hang a bell in this section."

Brother Goddard climbed farther into the upper section, and the others trailed after him.

"What are you going to do?" asked Brother Walker.

"Watch," said Brother Goddard.

"This is the clock tower," said John. "There are going to be clocks facing north, south, east and west."

Brother Goddard continued to the top of the narrow steps and pulled himself outside and up another ladder. Micah leaned out the window to see. Bright glare reflected off the silver dome.[4] Brother Goddard threw his leg over the walkway railing around the dome[5] and scaled the small ladder on the shiny roof. He tipped himself upside down and stood on his head near the spire.[6]

Everyone clapped.

"Wow!" said Alicia. "That's scary. I won't ever do that."

Micah ran his hand over the smooth wood of the shuttered windows. It felt soft and cool.

"Clear the way!" called someone from below.

"That's the tinsmith ready to set the angel in place," said John.

"Move aside," said the voice.

Micah looked down. He could see a man carrying a shiny gold angel with a trumpet in one hand and a book in the other. *It doesn't look like the angel Moroni on our temples,* thought Micah. *It's flying sideways with the trumpet in his hand. Our Angel Moroni stands straight up and blows the trumpet. This one's beautiful, though.*

"I need to get this set on top of the ball and spire,"

said the man. The angel tipped awkwardly in his hands.

"Oh," said Alicia. "Can we touch it?"

"Yes, but very carefully," said the man. "It's covered with gold leaf."

Alicia reached out to feel the trumpet.

The angel glittered in the bright sunlight, streaming through the window. Micah lightly stroked the gold. It felt cool. His hand reached out to the Book of Mormon and then the horn.[7]

"This is just like your dream," Micah said to John.

John smiled with tears in his eyes. "That was so long ago, but it seems like yesterday."

"The angel and the rest of the temple are very beautiful," said Micah. "Everyone has worked so hard to make it the best it can be. What about me? I wonder if I'll ever do anything like that to show the Lord I love Him?"

"You are already showing God how much you love Him by being yourself," said John.

"But I want to be better than I am right now," said Micah.

"We all want to improve," said John. "But God loves you like you are. We are all His greatest creations."

Micah moved aside for the tinsmith to pass. The angel wobbled in his arms as the smith angled through the men.

"Can we watch you put it up?" asked Alicia

"Watch from where you are," said the man. "It's dangerous on the roof. You could slip." He turned his head. "But I do need help holding the angel while I climb up to attach it."

"I want to help," said Micah. Here was his chance to show Heavenly Father he loved him by working on the temple.

"Fine," said the tinsmith. "Just watch your step."

Micah set his melon piece down and wiped his sticky hands on his pants.

"We need to tie a rope around your waist so you'll be safe," said Brother Richards.

"Good idea," said John. "Get me that rope over there in the corner."

Micah didn't want to have a rope tied around him. That was for babies, but if it was the only way he could put the angel up, he'd take it. He wanted to help. John knotted the rope around Micah's waist, and Micah stepped out onto the roof.

"See the ball and rod at the very top," the tinsmith said. "The flying angel with the book and trumpet will be fastened to the top of the rod."[8,9]

The tinsmith climbed ahead while Micah balanced the angel from beneath. The statue was heavier than it looked.

Micah glanced at the landscape surrounding the temple. The Mississippi River snaked along its course below him, moving slowly south. Green fields and trees spread out before him clear to the horizon. Micah took a deep breath. It was beautiful up here. Turning back to the angel, he tried to concentrate—stick to business.

Sunlight flashed off the gold plate, blinding him for a minute. He turned his head away from the glare. *I am so happy I can help with the angel*, thought Micah. *I can't wait to tell Dad about this blessing.*

The smith steadied his feet, grasped the angel from Micah, and faced the dome to attach it. Micah braced himself behind the smith, pulled the phone from his pocket, and clicked a picture.

"All finished," said the smith as he secured the angel in place.

Micah stepped backward but missed the rung on the ladder and slipped down to the observation landing. The phone flew out of his hands, pummeling toward the ground below. Micah watched it fly end over end headed for the ground. "No!" he yelled. "No, no, no." He peered over the edge. Workmen, horses, women bringing lunches all looked like tiny specks on the ground. The phone would smash for sure, and that would be the end of their trip. They would be stuck here forever.

"What happened?" asked the smith.

"My foot slid off the ladder," said Micah.

"Watch your step," called John.

Micah looked over the edge again. A horse whinnied and reared. Had the phone hit a horse and then shattered on the ground? That would be just his luck. He hurried down the dome steps. Pulling the rope back in, he climbed through the small door and clattered down the stairway. John untied Micah and wound the rope up to store in the corner.

"Wasn't it beautiful out there?" asked John.

"It was," said Micah, turning to Alicia, "but we're

sooo in trouble. When I slipped up on the roof, I had the pho . . . black box in my hand, and it flipped over the edge down to the ground."

"I'm sorry," said John. "What does this mean? You can't get home?"

"Probably," said Alicia.

Micah, Alicia, and John descended the wooden staircase. Workmen sawed and hammered everywhere.

Micah's hands trembled. "First I have to find the black box. I looked over the roof after it dropped, and I couldn't see what happened to it."

"Now we really have to use our faith," said Alicia, "like we did when the battery was dead."

What faith? thought Micah.

John put his hand on Micah's shoulder. "I'm sorry. You can stay with me if you can't get home. But Heavenly Father always helps me if I try to do what's right and listen to His promptings."

"I hope that'll work for us." Micah's shoulders felt crunched under a heavy weight. *I always seem to mess up,* he thought. *Why can't I ever just get it right?*

"Don't panic," said Alicia. "We just have to use our faith."

Micah wasn't sure about his faith. All he could do was hope. He rushed out the front door and down the steps to the side of the temple, where the phone had fallen. The workmen talked and laughed while the women handed out more watermelon slices. Children dashed under and around the ladders, wagons, and horses—stirring dust as they ran. They crawled under wooden scaffolding and between the stone mason's partially carved work.

"It's crazy around here," said Micah. "How are we going to find anything?"

"Say a prayer in your heart," said Alicia. "Let's see what we can do."

Micah didn't feel like praying. The phone was lost or ruined or both. He was always in trouble—always looking for a way to get home and never finding it.

Micah glanced up and saw Alicia's bowed head.

Micah lowered his head also. *Heavenly Father,* he pleaded, *please help me. I know I've made a lot of mistakes, but I promised Dad we would get back soon, and now he's worried. I need to take good care of Alicia, but sometimes it seems like she's taking care of me. Please, help my faith to be stronger.*

Micah took a deep breath and opened his eyes, feeling warm inside. He saw that Alicia had finished her prayer. "I think I should see if I can find the horse that reared after the phone dropped."

"Okay," said Alicia. "You ask, and I'll start searching."

15

WATERMELON JUICE

MICAH approached the driver nearest him. "Hello," he said. "Did your horse rear up for no reason a few minutes ago?"

"No," said the man, but I think Brother Hobart's did." The man pointed to a driver with a wagonload of lumber.

Micah hurried over to him. "Hello, Brother Hobart. Did your horse rear up a little while ago?"

"Why yes," said Brother Hobart. "I don't understand what happened."

"I might know why," said Micah. "I was up on the observation landing of the east tower, and I dropped something over the edge. It may have fallen here."

"Oh," said Brother Hobart. "That makes sense." He patted the horse's neck. "Charlie, here, is the most gentle animal around. Always trustworthy."

"I hope the horse . . . er . . . Charlie isn't hurt," said Micah.

"I'm sure he's fine," said Brother Hobart. "What was it that fell?"

"A little black box," said Micah.

"Oh, I saw that," said Brother Hobart. "Sister Carver's little boy picked it up and was running around with it, but he seems to have disappeared."

Oh, no! thought Micah. *What else can go wrong?*

Brother Hobart looked around. "Let's see . . . he's over there, eating a slice of watermelon." Brother Hobart pointed to a little boy about four or five years old.

Micah breathed a sigh of relief. *Thank you, Heavenly Father*, he thought.

Sister Carver's little boy had the phone all right and was smushing it into his slice of watermelon. He pounded it over and over. *Oh no*, thought Micah. *The phone is ruined for sure. How will I ever get the watermelon juice out of it?*

"Look, Ma," the little boy said. "I'm making watermelon juice just like you make grape juice."

Micah wanted to grab the phone away from the little kid, but that wasn't polite. He should ask the boy's mother first. She was talking to a woman whose little girl hung on her skirts, crying.

Alicia walked up and shrugged her shoulders. She hadn't found anything.

Micah pointed to the phone.

Alicia nodded.

"Sister Carver," said Micah, "I'm sorry to disturb you, but your boy has my black box."

"Oh, I apologize," said Sister Carver. "I wonder how he got a hold of it."

"It's my fault," said Micah. "I dropped it."

"Joshua," said Sister Carver, "give the boy his box."

"No," Joshua said. "It's mine."

"We don't take things that don't belong to us," said Sister Carver to Joshua.

"It's mine," Joshua said again. "It fell off the horse."

Sister Carver looked at Micah.

He felt his face getting hot. "Joshua's right. I was on the roof and dropped the box. It must have landed on the horse."

"Look," said Alicia to Joshua, wiping the dust off a piece of stone shaped like a stick and handing it to him. "This will make a better juicer than the black box." She drummed the stone-stick into one end of his watermelon, making it juicy and pressed a little ditch in the rind so the liquid could run out. She helped Joshua tip the juice to his mouth. "Here's your new watermelon drink."

He slurped it up, and Alicia clapped for him. "Good for you."

Joshua dropped the phone on the ground and began to hit the watermelon with the stone-stick in earnest, stopping to gulp the juice cradled in the rind.

"Thanks," said Micah to Sister Carver.

"No, thank you," said Sister Carver. "Great idea. We'll have watermelon juice with supper."

Micah picked up the phone, and he and Alicia hurried down the hill away from the crowd.

"Let's go to the Mississippi," said Micah, "and see if we can clean up this sticky mess."

Down by the river Micah found a fallen log that they could sit on. Alicia dipped a handkerchief from her pocket into the water.

Micah handed her the phone, and she wiped off the outside. She swiped the screen, but the phone remained dark. Micah took the back off, and Alicia carefully blotted the moisture from the battery and the memory card.

"Let me rinse the hanky and clean out the inside," said Alicia. She dipped it in the river and squeezed the extra water out before she scoured the phone inside and out again.

Micah put the phone back together and touched the screen.

Nothing.

"Maybe it needs to dry," said Micah, opening up the back and leaving the phone in the sun. In a few minutes he put it back together, but still nothing. "What are we going to do?"

"Maybe we're stuck here forever, said Alicia. "I'm really scared—all because of a little piece of watermelon."

Micah wrinkled his brow. "How can watermelon completely destroy our chance to get back home? Well, *and* slipping on the ladder and dropping the phone."

"We have to have faith. Let's pray," said Alicia.

"I'll say it this time."

Micah prayed the phone would work. He made sure the memory card and battery were in tight and swiped the phone again.

It lit up.

I DON'T APPRECIATE BEING FULL OF WATERMELON JUICE.

"Oh," said Micah, feeling relieved. "Heavenly Father really did bless us. I can't believe the phone is working. Faith *really* works."

I DO *NOT* LIKE BEING USED AS A HAMMER BY A LITTLE KID.

"I'm so sorry," said Micah. "But I'm very happy you're working."

YOU'RE LUCKY I LANDED ON A HORSE. OTHERWISE I'D BE SMASHED TO PIECES, AND YOU WOULD BE STUCK HERE.

"I know," said Micah. "I'm really sorry, and I'm so happy you're working."

YOU ALREADY SAID THAT.

"Can't I say it again? I *am* really happy."

I GUESS. PLEASE HANG ON TO ME FROM NOW ON.

"I will," Micah said to the phone.

ON SECOND THOUGHT, LET ALICIA KEEP TRACK OF ME FOR THE REST OF THE JOURNEY.

Alicia smiled.

"I guess I deserve that," said Micah. He didn't care who held the phone. "At least we have a chance to get home now."

"We should find John and tell him we're going home," said Alicia.

GOOD IDEA, said the phone. I'LL TAKE YOU.

Blackness enveloped them, and they landed on the first floor of the temple, where John was sanding a chair leg. He saw them and hurried over.

"Did you find the box?" he asked.

"Yes," said Micah. "Heavenly Father blesses me even when I mess up."

"He does do that," said John. "We all make mistakes at times."

"The final piece of the puzzle is the angel that you saw in your dream, flying through the heavens with a trumpet," said Alicia.

"I'm so grateful Heavenly Father let me see that

angel," said John. "The gospel will be preached to all the world."

"In our day, missionaries learn different languages and serve in almost every country," said Micah.

"What a blessing," said John. "Joseph Smith revealed that everyone would hear the gospel in his own language."[1]

"Thanks for helping me have faith," said Micah.

"Never forget," said John, "someday you'll be a missionary and baptize by the power of the priesthood. The priesthood you hold 'is living power.'"[2]

"Living power." Micah stood tall. Strength tingled through his body. He would tell his deacons quorum if they ever got home. "Living power."

Alicia hugged John. "Thanks for the big words."

"And the funny accent," said John.

"I love you," said Alicia.

"I love you too," said John.

Alicia and Micah walked out of the temple and into the twilight, watching the pink clouds of the sunset reflect on the river.

The phone lit up: TEXT YOUR JOURNALS.

Micah texted:

I NEED TO HAVE MORE FAITH. I DROPPED THE PHONE AND THOUGHT WE WERE STUCK, BUT HEAVENLY FATHER BLESSES US. IT TOOK A LOT OF WORK TO BUILD THE TEMPLE. I WANT TO WORK HARD FOR HEAVENLY FATHER DURING MY LIFE.

He pushed SEND.

Alicia typed:

I AM IN CHARGE OF THE PHONE NOW. THE PHONE LIKES ME BECAUSE I DIDN'T DROP IT. I WANT TO BE THE BEST I CAN BE. JOHN SAYS GOD LOVES ME NO MATTER WHAT.

She sent her text.

Alicia pressed the screen, and the wheel appeared. The picture of the angel slid into the center and a golden glow lit up the wheel.

SCRIPTURE PICTURE COMPLETE

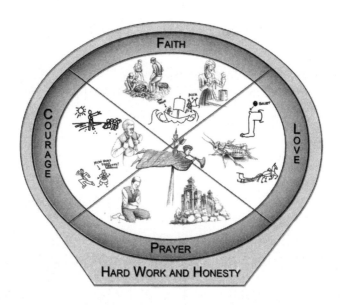

CONGRATULATIONS, MICAH AND ALICIA. JOURNEY CONCLUDED.

"A circle," said Alicia. "Faith, Courage, Love, and Prayer."

"With an angel sending a message to all the world in the center," said Micah.

YOU CAN PRINT THE CIRCLE WHEN YOU GET
HOME AS A REMINDER OF YOUR JOURNEY.

"Thanks," said Alicia. "I'll hang it in my room."

Alicia pressed PRESENT, and blackness enfolded
them. They tumbled through time and space, landing
in front of their house by the rock under the pine tree.

Micah raised his hand in a high five. "Beat you to
the house." He ran ahead before she could slap his palm.

"I'm not racing," said Alicia, walking behind him.
She twirled her necklace around her finger and admired
her CTR ring in the sun. Her shorts and flip-flops felt
so comfortable.

Dad rushed out the back door. "You're home! I've
been so worried. I was afraid you were gone forever—
low battery and all!"

"We didn't think we were going to get home either,"
said Alicia, giving him a hug.

"How on earth did you recharge it?" Dad asked,
stroking Alicia's hair.

"Now, that's a story," said Micah. "But let's start
from the beginning."

"Why couldn't you come with us?" asked Alicia.

"It was my own mistake," said Dad. "I wanted to try
out a new antitheft device so I put it on this phone, and
then I forgot about it."

"Antitheft," said Micah. "What does that mean?"

"It simply means that since you and Alicia were the
first to use the phone, no one else was authorized to
employ the time travel but you."

"That makes sense," said Micah.

The phone buzzed and then lit up: I'VE BEEN FRIED

LIKE A FISH, THROWN OFF A BUILDING, USED AS A HAMMER, AND DRENCHED IN JUICE.

"Wow," said Dad.

I DESERVE A CLEAN-UP JOB IF WE'RE GOING TO HAVE ANY MORE ADVENTURES.

"Stay home for a while," said Dad.

"We need to," said Micah. "I want time to be thankful for the things I have."

"Like what?" asked Dad.

"The fridge," said Micah, thinking of John's small ice box in Nauvoo.

"And not eating burned crickets," said Alicia.

"Or wearing girl's clothes," said Micah, remembering France.

"What?" asked Dad.

Alicia laughed. "Come on, Dad. Let's get our journals off the email and we'll tell you all about it."

MICAH'S JOURNAL

JOHN MUST BE FROM A RICH FAMILY. HE HAS SHIRTS WITH LACE. COLLARS AND PUFFY SLEEVES. I HAD TO TUCK MY SHIRT IN. PLAYED WAR AGAINST THE SCOTS. FUN, FUN, FUN.

PRAYED WITH A PROPHET. MUSIC HELPS ME FEEL THE SPIRIT. JOHN KNOWS HE'S COMING TO AMERICA. PRAYED TO GET HOME. IS HEAVENLY FATHER LISTENING? WILL HE ANSWER MY PRAYERS?

PIONEERS HAD A HARD TIME CROSSING THE OCEAN. STORMS ARE SCARY. JOHN IS FAITHFUL. HE KNOWS GOD WILL PROTECT HIM . . . DO I KNOW IF GOD WILL PROTECT ME?

JOHN ALMOST GOT TARRED AND FEATHERED. HE HAD COURAGE TO PREACH ANYWAY. FREEDOM DOESN'T MEAN YOU HAVE THE RIGHT TO HURT OTHER PEOPLE. I WANT TO BE KIND TO OTHERS.

JOHN GOT SHOT FIVE TIMES, AND HE'S ALIVE. GOD PROTECTED HIM. WE TOOK CARE OF HIM FOR THE AFTERNOON. I'M GLAD I COULD HELP. I LOVE THE PROPHET JOSEPH SMITH.

HELPED BUILD A HOUSE, RODE A HORSE, MET SOME INDIANS. THEY SHOWED US HOT TO FIND FOOD THAT GROWS IN THE WILD. WE DIDN'T EVEN HAVE TO BUY IT AT THE STORE. MY FAITH IS WEAK. HOW DO I GET STRONGER FAITH?

HEAVENLY FATHER BLESSED US TO GET AWAY FROM THE POLICE IN PARIS. BATTERY ON THE PHONE WENT DEAD. PRAYED. GOD BLESSED US TO GET IT STARTED AGAIN. MY FAITH IS STRONGER.

WE HAVE TO SOLVE THIS PUZZLE YOU PUT ON THE PHONE BEFORE WE CAN GET HOME. WILL COME AS SOON AS WE CAN.

TAUGHT THE BOYS ABOUT HONESTY AND TITHING. IT FEELS GOOD TO HELP A PROPHET. I'M GLAD I COULD GO TO THE FIRST PRIMARY MEETING. JOHN SAYS PRIMARY TEACHES US ABOUT FAITH.

I NEED TO LISTEN AND HAVE MORE FAITH. I FELT THE SPIRIT IN THE TEMPLE DEDICATION. I LOVE BEING IN THE TEMPLE.

I NEED TO HAVE MORE FAITH. I DROPPED THE PHONE AND THOUGHT WE WERE STUCK, BUT HEAVENLY FATHER BLESSED US. IT TOOK A LOT OF WORK TO BUILD THE TEMPLE. I WANT TO WORK HARD DURING MY LIFE.

ALICIA'S JOURNAL

JOHN IS KIND. HE TOLD ME TO PICK BLACKBERRIES, AND HE WANTED TO SHARE HIS LUNCH WITH ME. I LOVED THE CASTLE RUINS, ATE BERRIES, DREAMED OF BEAUTIFUL JEWEL NECKLACES. CASTLE ECHOES ARE TOO LOUD FOR ME. MISSED THE PICNIC AND JAM SANDWICHES.

JOHN LIKES TO PRAY. SO DO I. HE LISTENS TO HEAVENLY FATHER. I WILL TRY TO LISTEN TO WHAT HEAVENLY FATHER TELLS ME.

FRIGHTENED BY STORM. ALMOST DROWNED. MICAH SAVED ME. GOD SAVED JOHN. MAYBE GOD SAVED BOTH OF US. . . . DO I HAVE ENOUGH FAITH?

LEONORA IS A FANCY LADY. SHE WORE A BEAUTIFUL PIN. JOHN SPEAKS LIKE A PROPHET OF GOD. I FELT THE HOLY GHOST WHEN HE TALKED. JOHN ISN'T AFRAID TO STAND UP FOR THE CHURCH. I WANT TO BE BRAVE LIKE HE IS. I DON'T LIKE TAR AND FEATHERING. I CAN BE UNDERSTANDING OF PEOPLE WHO ARE DIFFERENT THAN ME.

JOHN IS GETTING BETTER, BUT HE STILL LOOKS PALE. WE FED HIM VEGGIES. HE LOVES JOSEPH SMITH, AND SO DO I. LEONORA VISITED SISTER EMMA. SHE IS SAD THAT JOSEPH DIED. I AM TOO.

JOHN HEALED AN INDIAN BOY FROM THE MEASLES. THE MEASLES. THE INDIANS BROUGHT JOHN GIFTS OF FOOD. JOHN WAS THANKFUL BECAUSE HIS FAMILY WOULDN'T STARVE. INDIAN FOOD IS GROSS. PLEASE TAKE ME HOME.

JOHN GOT IN TROUBLE FOR PREACHING, BUT NONE OF US WENT TO JAIL. PHONE QUIT WORKING. I WAS SCARED AND FELT SORRY FOR MYSELF. WE PRAYED, AND HEAVENLY FATHER SENT AN OLD WOMAN TO BE OUR FRIEND. WE RECHARGED THE SOLAR BATTERY WITH THE SUN.

I DON'T WANT TO RUN AFTER WAGONS IN THE STREET. IT'S TOO SCARY. I HAD FUN DIPPING CANDLES. I WENT TO THE FIRST PRIMARY MEETING. I LOVE PRIMARY.

I'M GOING TO THE TEMPLE AS SOON AS I'M TWELVE. ANGELS MAY BE THERE WITH ME. I LOVE THE TEMPLE. JOHN IS A PROPHET OF GOD. I'M THANKFUL FOR HIM.

I AM IN CHARGE OF THE PHONE NOW. THE PHONE LIKES ME BECAUSE I DIDN'T DROP IT. I WANT TO BE THE BEST I CAN BE. JOHN SAYS GOD LOVES ME NO MATTER WHAT. I WANT TO BELIEVE THAT'S TRUE.

ACKNOWLEDGMENTS

I AM grateful to my husband and children for their unfailing love and support. Thanks to my critique group for helping me become a better writer: Margot Hovley, Marion Jensen, Chris Miller, Kendra Fowler, Cory Webb, Jeanette Wright, and Ken Lee. Rosalie Ledezma's artwork is wonderful. I feel honored that she would illustrate my book.

Thanks to Mary Jane Woodger for writing the book's foreword. Her support and kindness in taking time for this project will be ever appreciated. She brings an element of credence and scholarship to the work because she edited *Champion of Liberty: John Taylor* (Salt Lake City: Deseret Book, 2009). I will ever be grateful for her help.

 # NOTES

CHAPTER 1

1. "The Pele Towers of Cumbria," http://www.visitcumbria.com/pele.htm

CHAPTER 2

1. Paul Thomas Smith, *Presidents of the Church: John Taylor*, ed. Leonard J. Arrington (Salt Lake City: Deseret Book, Salt Lake City, 1986), 77.

2. B. H. Roberts, *The Life of John Taylor* (Salt Lake City: Bookcraft, 1963), 26-27.

3. Ibid., 27-28, as cited in *Teachings of the Presidents of the Church: John Taylor* (Salt Lake City: The Church of Jesus Christ of Latter-day Saints, 2001), xii.

4. Roberts, *The Life of John Taylor*, 28.

5. *Presidents of the Church: John Taylor*, 77.

CHAPTER 3

1. Historical summary, as cited in *Teachings of the Presidents of the Church: John Taylor*, vii–viii.

2. Roberts, *The Life of John Taylor*, 28

3. Ibid., 29.

CHAPTER 4

1. Roberts, *The Life of John Taylor*, 38.

2. Ibid., 87.

3. Ibid., 53–55.

4. Samuel W. Taylor, *The Last Pioneer: John Taylor, A Mormon Prophet* (Salt Lake City: Signature Books, 1999), 52.

CHAPTER 5

1. Smith, *Presidents of the Church: John Taylor*, 90-91.
2. Ibid., 53.
3. Ibid., 38; Doctrine and Covenants 135:4.
4. Roberts, *The Life of John Taylor*, 130–151

CHAPTER 6

1. Bible Dictionary, 749, 741.
2. Roberts, *The Life of John Taylor*, 149.
3. Ibid., 150.
4. Doctrine and Covenants 135:1, 3, 6.

CHAPTER 7

1. Taylor, *The Last Pioneer: John Taylor, A Mormon Prophet*, 138–139.

CHAPTER 8

1. Smith, *Presidents of the Church: John Taylor*, 99.
2. Taylor, *The Last Pioneer: John Taylor, A Mormon Prophet*, 157–158.
3. Roberts, *The Life of John Taylor*, 28.

CHAPTER 9

1. Wikipedia, "Burning Glass"

CHAPTER 10

1. J. Lewis Taylor "John Taylor: Family Man," in *Champion of Liberty: John Taylor*, ed. Mary Jane Woodger (Salt Lake City: Deseret Book, 2009), 205.
2. 2 Samuel 12:6; Luke 19:8.
3. Taylor, "John Taylor: Family Man," *Champion of Liberty: John Taylor*, 204-205.
4. Julia Neville Taylor, "An Interview with Ezra Oakley Taylor, Son of President John Taylor," (Church History Department Archives, n.d.) microfilm, 2, as cited in *Teachings of the Presidents of the Church: John Taylor* (Salt Lake City: The Church of

Jesus Christ of Latter-day Saints, 2001), xix.

5. Susan Arrington Madsen, *The Lord Needed a Prophet,* (Salt Lake City: Deseret Book, 1996), 56.

6. Taylor, "John Taylor: Family Man," *Champion of Liberty John Taylor,* 206.

7. James Montgomery, "A Poor Wayfaring Man of Grief," *Hymns* (Salt Lake City: The Church of Jesus Christ of Latter-day Saints), 29-30.

8. William E. Berrett, *The Restored Church* (Salt Lake City: Deseret Book, 1961), 58.

9. Wilford Woodruff, *History of His Life and Labors,* ed. Matthias F. Cowley (Salt Lake City: Bookcraft, 1964), 468–469.

10. John Taylor, *Deseret News: Semi-Weekly,* December 16, 1873, 1, as cited in *Teachings of the Presidents of the Church: John Taylor,* 61.

CHAPTER 11

1. Naomi M. Shumway, "'Foundation for the Future': A Conversation with Naomi M. Shumway, General President of the Primary," *Ensign,* April 1978, 33.

2. Ibid.

3. 1870 US Census, Utah Territory, Davis County, Farmington City, July 28, 1870, p. 17, line 7.

4. Carol Cornwall Madsen, Church Historical Department, *Church News,* August 26, 1978, 11.

CHAPTER 12

1. Carol Cornwall Madsen, Church Historical Department, *Church News,* August 26, 1978, 11.

2. Shumway, "Foundation for the Future."

3. "The Children's Friend," *Friend,* January 1978, 47.

4. Ibid., 48.

5. *Sing with Me: Songs for Children,* Salt Lake City: Deseret Book Company, 1969, B-24–25.

6. "The Children's Friend," 47.

7. "The Joseph Smith Papers," BYUtv documentary, aired May 8, 2011.

CHAPTER 13

1. Nolan P. Olsen, *Logan Temple: The First 100 Years* (Providence, UT: Keith W. Watkins and Sons, 1978), 135.
2. Ibid., 152–153.
3. Ibid., 139
4. Ibid., 146–147
5. Ibid., 149
6. Ibid.

CHAPTER 14

1. Don F. Colvin, *Nauvoo Temple: A Story of Faith* (American Fork, UT: Covenant Communications, 2002), 249.
2. Matthew S. McBride, *A House for the Most High: The Story of the Original Nauvoo Temple* (Salt Lake City: Greg Kofford Books, 2006), 228.
3. Ibid.
4. Colvin, *Nauvoo Temple: A Story of Faith*, 144
5. Ibid. 213
6. McBride, *A House for the Most High: The Story of the Original Nauvoo Temple*, 228.
7. Colvin, *Nauvoo Temple: A Story of Faith*, 147
8. Ibid., 144
9. Ibid. The Tinners Association was working on the angel at this time. The angel was not placed on top of the temple until February 1846, just a few weeks before the Saints were driven from Nauvoo. The tinsmith places the statue during the summer of 1845 to expedite the story.

CHAPTER 15

1. Doctrine and Covenants 90:11
2. *The Gospel Kingdom*, sel. G. Homer Durham (1943), 127, as cited in *Teachings of the Presidents of the Church: John Taylor*, 117.

DISCUSSION QUESTIONS

CHAPTER 1: What did Alicia like about England? What didn't she like? What were Micah's favorite things about the English countryside? What did he dislike? Would you like to visit England? Why or why not?

CHAPTER 2: What happened when John asked his friends to pray with him? How did Micah and Alicia feel when they prayed with John? What did John see in his dream? Did he know what it meant when he was young before he joined the Church?

CHAPTER 3: How did Micah and Alicia know that John had faith? Did they think their faith was as strong as John's? How did John come to have such great faith? What do we need to do to have faith like John's?

CHAPTER 4: John showed courage when he spoke to the people. What did he tell them about freedom? Does freedom mean we have the right to hurt others? Alicia really liked meeting Leonora, John's wife. What do you think Alicia admired most about Leonora? What do you like best about her?

CHAPTER 5: Was it hard for John to talk about being with Joseph Smith in Carthage jail when the Prophet was killed? How did Alicia and Micah help take care of John? What was Micah thankful for?

CHAPTER 6: What is a martyr? Name several martyrs. Was Joseph Smith a martyr? How did Micah feel when he read what John had written about Joseph Smith? How do those words make you feel? How do you feel about Joseph Smith?

CHAPTER 7: How did Chief Little Face feel about the blessing John gave his son? What did he do to show how he felt? Did the pioneers have a lot of food when they first arrived in the Salt Lake Valley? How did the Indians help them? Would you like to eat burned, ground up crickets? How are you a pioneer today?

CHAPTER 8: How did Micah like his French clothes? What did Alicia think of hers? How did John escape the police? How did the old woman cook her fish?

CHAPTER 9: Could the kids recharge the battery the same way the woman cooked the fish? Why? How did they recharge the battery? What was Micah grateful for after cooking his fish for breakfast? How did John show his courage when he left Paris, France?

CHAPTER 10: What did John do when his sons sold the neighbor's chickens? What did John do when his children didn't take time to plant the garden in straight rows? How did John teach them to work hard and be honest? What will help you remember to be honest? What did John do when he saw Martin Harris in the back of the tabernacle? How would you feel if you saw one of the witnesses to the Book of Mormon?

CHAPTER 11: Why was John worried about the boys and girls in Farmington, Utah? What did Bishop Hess and Sister Rogers want to do? What did Micah do when he found the boys stealing melons? What would you have done?

CHAPTER 12: Why was hitching rides on the back of wagons dangerous? How did Alicia make friends with the girls? What did Alicia suggest the girls do instead of snagging rides on wagons? Would you catch a ride on the back of a wagon? Why? Describe the first Primary. How is Primary different today?

CHAPTER 13: Why were Arabella and Adam feeling happy? Would you be happy if you were doing the same thing? What did Arabella cook that was so delicious? Do you like to cook? What do you like to make? Have you ever been to a temple open house? Have you been to a temple dedication? How did you feel when you were there? How did Alicia and Micah feel about leaving John? How would you feel?

CHAPTER 14: What was everyone eating at the Nauvoo temple site? What did Brother Goddard do? Would you do that? Why or why not? How did Micah feel when he dropped the phone? What did John tell him?

CHAPTER 15: What happened to the phone after Micah dropped it? How did Alicia save the day? Were their prayers answered? Have you had your prayers answered? When and how? How does God feel about us even if we make mistakes?

ABOUT THE AUTHOR

CHRISTY Monson has always loved pioneer history, especially stories of the prophets. She received her bachelor's degree from Utah State University, and a master's degree from the University of Nevada, Las Vegas. After her six children were raised, she established a successful marriage and family therapy practice. She has published articles in the *Ensign*, in the *Friend*, and in other children's periodicals. She and her husband, Robert, live in Ogden, Utah.